PUFFIN BOOKS

Siobhán Parkinson is one of Ireland's best-known authors for children and teenagers, and she has won numerous awards for her writing. Her books have been translated into many languages, from Danish to Thai – even ones where they translate your name as well as your book, so somewhere in Central Europe there are books by a person called Šivena Parkinsona.

She is joint editor of *Bookbird*, an international journal on children's literature, and when she is not writing stories or pretending to be Šivena Parkinsona, she visits schools and works with children on their writing projects. Siobhán lives in Dublin with her husband and grown-up son.

Puffin books by Siobhán Parkinson

SECOND FIDDLE
SOMETHING INVISIBLE
BLUE LIKE FRIDAY

Blue Like Friday

SIOBHÁN PARKINSON

PUFFIN

PUFFIN BOOKS

Published by the Penguin Group
Penguin Books Ltd, 80 Strand, London WC2R ORL, England
Penguin Group (USA) Inc., 375 Hudson Street, New York, New York 10014, USA
Penguin Group (Canada), 90 Elignton Avenue East, Suite 700, Toronto, Ontario, Canada M4P 2Y3
(a division of Pearson Penguin Canada Inc.)
Penguin Ireland, 25 St Stephen's Green, Dublin 2, Ireland (a division of Penguin Books Ltd)
Penguin Group (Australia), 250 Camberwell Road, Camberwell, Victoria 3124, Australia
(a division of Pearson Australia Group Pty Ltd)
Penguin Books India Pvt Ltd, 11 Community Centre, Panchsheel Park, New Delhi – 110 017, India
Penguin Group (NZ), 67 Apollo Drive, Rosedale, North Shore 0632, New Zealand
(a division of Pearson New Zealand Ltd)
Penguin Books (South Africa) (Pty) Ltd, 24 Sturdee Avenue, Rosebank, Johannesburg 2196, South Africa

Penguin Books Ltd, Registered Offices: 80 Strand, London WC2R ORL, England

penguin.com

First published 2007
1

Typeset in Baskerville MT by Palimpsest Book Production Limited,
Grangemouth, Stirlingshire

Made and printed in England by Clays Ltd, St Ives plc

British Library Cataloguing in Publication Data
A CIP catalogue record for this book is available from the British Library

ISBN 978-0-141-32094-6

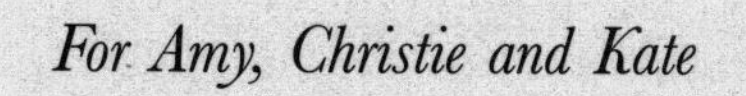
For Amy, Christie and Kate

Chapter 1

The thing is, blue is not really a great colour for a kite, is it?

'I mean, think about it,' I said to Hal. 'Where does a kite spend its time?'

He stared at me in that goofy way he has. I know he is not really goofy, just thinking about something else, but he does a very good impression of goofy just the same.

'Its *working* time, Hal,' I explained. 'When it's doing its stuff, like.'

We were in Hal's garage. His mother had started to have it converted into a playroom for Hal, but she'd lost interest halfway through – typical, according to Hal, and he throws his eyes up as he says it – and the conversion never got finished, so it was sort of stuck halfway between a garage and a room: there was lino on the floor like in a room, but it still had a garage up-and-over door.

Hal said nothing. He is good at saying nothing. He has plenty to say for himself when he wants to, but he can do silence like no one else I know. I could *shake* him!

But I didn't shake him. Instead, I answered my own question. 'In the sky, right? And,' I went on, 'what colour is the sky?'

Well, you can see where that argument was going, can't you? But Hal just said – wait for it! – Hal said the kite had to be blue because of Friday being blue. I *ask* you!

'Friday is not blue, Hal,' I said patiently. 'Friday is just a day.'

'It's blue,' said Hal. He stopped for a bit and then he said, 'It's a light, pretty blue. With frills.'

I do try to understand Hal, but it's not easy.

'Pass me the glue,' he went on. 'Careful!' he said then, as I went to pick it up. 'Make sure you don't get it on your fingers; it's very strong. It'd strip your skin off as fast as look at you.'

'It's only a tube of glue, Hal,' I said, passing it to him. 'It doesn't *look* at people.'

'And tangy,' Hal added.

'What?' I yelped. 'Have you been *licking* it? I thought you said it would strip your skin off.' Then I had a terrible thought. 'Or *sniffing* it? Hal, you shouldn't do that, it's dangerous. Your nose falls off and your brain goes to mush and you die.'

That might have been a bit of an exaggeration, and I have promised my mother I will try not to exaggerate so much, but you probably do die in the end, and I'm sure it's not a dignified death, all slobbering with no nose to speak of.

'Not the glue,' said Hal. 'Friday.'

He can be clear as mud, that boy.

'I don't get it, Hal,' I said.

'I mean, it's Friday that's tangy,' Hal said. 'It's sort of lemony, only sweet, like lemon sherbet.'

To you (I hope) and me, Friday is the day after Thursday – right? – and the day the weekend begins, yippee! But if you're Hal, it seems that Friday is a bag of blue lemon sherbet. How weird is that?

I started to unwind my sweatshirt from round my waist so I could put it on. It was kind of draughty in Hal's not-really-a-garage-but-not-quite-a-room.

'Explain, Hal,' I said as I put on my sweatshirt. 'Explain about Friday being blue.'

Hal said nothing.

'Can you *he-ear* me?' I asked, knocking on his forehead. 'Anybody *ho-ome*? *How* is Friday blue?'

'In my head,' said Hal, pushing me away.

The inside of Hal's head has to be the weirdest place.

'When I think Friday,' he said, 'I see blue. That's all.'

I wriggled my cold toes in my sandals and wished I'd worn runners and socks. 'You live in your head, that's the problem,' I told him.

He looked at me blankly for a moment and then he sort of waved his hands about and said, 'But where else would I live?'

Which more or less proved my point, since the obvious answer to that is, 'In the real world, with the rest of us.' I tried to imagine what it must be like to think that Friday is blue, but I couldn't.

'I might say Friday has a rosy glow myself,' I said after a while. 'But that's a metaphor. Have you heard of metaphors, Hal?'

We did metaphors in English last term, and I think they are cool, but I don't think Hal always listens in class. He's usually doodling or colouring in. So he could easily have missed the metaphors.

'Hmm,' said Hal, holding up the frame of the kite and turning it round and round and looking at it from different angles. 'I s'ppose.'

I could see that he wasn't really listening.

'It's when you say something is something else,' I explained helpfully, 'only you don't mean it's actually something else; it's just that a bit of the meaning of the something else sort of rubs off on the something you first thought of.'

Hal's mouth dropped open. He must have been listening after all. He didn't look so marvellous with his mouth hanging open. He has quite a nice face, most of the time. Ordinary, but sort of roundy and smiley and with a lot of fringe and eyebrow.

While I am at it, I should tell you that my face

is fairly ordinary too, roundy and freckly, and my hair is curly and pale. I used to say 'blonde', but my dad laughed at me and said, 'You mean hay-coloured,' which I thought didn't sound very grand, so now I describe it as 'pale'. That's more interesting than 'blonde' anyway. It drives me mad, though, my hair, because it curls up all by itself into little corkscrews. My so-called friend Rosemarie lent me her hair-straighteners once, but it came out all crinkly instead of straight, and that was worse than actual curls, so I have given up on that.

'So you see, when I say Friday has a rosy glow,' I said to Hal, 'I don't mean that it's *really* pink or smells sweet or even that it's like a rose; I just mean there is something nice about Friday. See?'

'No,' said Hal.

'Only of course,' I went on, 'you can't say things are "nice" because that is a no-no word. You have to use a metaphor instead. That's how poetry works. Poets never say things are nice. Have you noticed that, Hal? That's why they are poets and we are not. They always find better ways to say ordinary things. That's what poetry is *for*.'

'Hmm,' said Hal.

He didn't sound very interested in my explanation about metaphors and poems. He listens more slowly than I talk, that's the trouble.

'Things usually aren't nice, though, are they?' he said then.

'They *are*,' I said. 'I think they are. Friday is anyway, and chocolate cake and kittens and sunshine. You just have to think about the right kind of things; that's how you make yourself happy.'

'Hmm,' he said again and he didn't sound very cheerful.

Chapter 2

'Everyone doesn't have to be *normal*, Olivia,' my mum was always saying when I tried to explain about Hal and how weird he could be sometimes. 'And, of course, Hal . . . Well, poor Hal.'

She meant about Hal not having a father. I mean, he did have a father once, but it was a long time ago – I don't remember him anyway, though I suppose I must have known him when I was small, because Hal and I have been friends *forever*.

She means well, I know, my mum, but it's as if all she can see when she looks at Hal is 'that poor fatherless boy'. That's typical of adults. They feel bad about some awful thing that's happened to a person, and they feel so bad about it that when they look at the person, all they see is the Awful Thing and they forget about the person themself. It's as if the person has *become* the Awful Thing, and they don't even notice the other things about them, like their views on Fridays or their kite-making skills or anything.

'Anyway, there's no such thing as normal,' my dad added. (My dad is a political economist, by the way. Do *not* ask me what that means, because all I know is that it seems to mean he could talk gobbledygook for Ireland.)

I don't know why they were banging on about normalness anyway. I never said Hal wasn't normal. I just said he was a bit weird. Lots of normal people have weird sides to them.

My mum, now, is normal, but she's also very psychological. She is not actually a psychologist, not professionally; it's more a sort of hobby. What she actually does is she works in a clinic for people who have had strokes, same as Hal's mum does. That's how we know Hal's family – I mean apart from Hal and me being in the same class at school – our mums work together. We've been friends since preschool, me and Hal. I suppose we are sort of stuck with each other.

She listens to those programmes on the radio, my mum, where all these people ring up who think that the problems of the world all come from horrible things that happened in the past that have made people unhappy, and then because they are unhappy they are mean, and then they do more horrible things to other people and make *them* unhappy, and so it goes on. That part is probably true, up to a point, but people like my mum think that if you could just stop the world spinning round for a few minutes, or maybe more like for about ten years, and let them get their sleeves rolled up and sort things out, then we could all start again from scratch, like Adam and Eve, only this time we'd know about the snake, and we wouldn't listen to it, and then everything would be fine.

If you ask me, those people are bonkers, because an awful lot of the problems in the world have nothing to do with a few nasty things that you could just poke out with a scalpel before sewing everything back together again. Take measles, for example. Or mosquitoes. Or the way you get blisters when you wear new shoes. Measles just *are* measles, and they aren't caused by someone being horrible to someone. I tried to explain this to my mum and she said, well, if we were all nicer to each other, we would send anti-measles vaccine all over the world and then no one would ever get the measles again. But that doesn't explain how measles got here in the first place, does it?

And anyway, if we got rid of measles, there'd be something else. Bird flu or tsunamis. There just *is* bad stuff, like Hal not having a dad any more, and we just have to get on with it, because no matter how many things you put right in the world, there's always other stuff left over. Like when you do division with funny numbers and you are left with a remnant. No, that's not the word. A remainder. That's it.

Hal isn't bonkers, by the way, only a bit weird. But he has one thing in common with my mother (and she's a bit dippy, I have to say, at times). He has these ideas about how you could put things *right*. He thought that if he could just get rid of this one key person from his life, then things would all go back to the way they were before and he'd be happy and everything would be rosy in the garden – a sort of permanent Friday with Adam and Eve and no snakes.

I think maybe boys have a different way of looking at things. That could be it.

Chapter 3

Hal got the idea for the kite one day when we were on the Low Strand. I don't know why they call it that, because it's not as if there is a High Strand. Don't ask me why. I didn't invent the geography; I just live here.

'Here' is Balnamara and it's a long way from anywhere, my mother always says, which is ridiculous, because every place is just beside the place next to it, isn't it, no matter where it is? What she means is, it's a long way from Dublin, which is her idea of somewhere. We have a set of traffic lights on the main street, though, and a hospital on the other side of town from the strand. There's a golf club just outside town, and a new Thai restaurant in the Market Square, and the old court house has been turned into a swanky new arts centre with a coffee shop where you can have all fancy coffees in tall glasses, and there's a big shopping centre with a pay-and-display car park. It is not exactly the back of beyond.

The Low Strand is pretty low, I suppose. It is one of those strands that gets totally engulfed when the tide comes in, with water right up to the sea wall. I suppose that is the reason it is only a strand and not a beach. It is not very golden or good to lie on, but is large and flat and grey and damp-to-sloppy. The tide seems to be mostly out, and then there's no sign of the sea at all, except for a seaweedy tang on the air and lukewarm little puddles in the gloopy sand, good for splashing in.

It was summertime, or nearly, or we wouldn't have been on the Low Strand in the first place, but it was that bit of summer before the holidays start, a sort of in-between time. It was in-between weather too, not warm like summer should be, but not so cold you'd need a coat. Sort of undecided.

The tide was coming lazily in, and we'd been paddling, me and Hal. The water wasn't deep enough to swim in, because the tide was only half in, and anyway we aren't allowed to swim unless we have a parent with us, even if there is a lifeguard, which is just so yawn-making, but there you go; that's just one of those ways parents (even fairly nice ones) oppress us kids. They call it being responsible. I call it being a pain.

There were these young kids on the strand as well as us. I don't know who let *them* out on their own; they were only about four. Well, seven, maybe, or eight at the most. There were three or four of them, all together, and they had this kite, a multicoloured one with a face, quite funny, with mad purple streamers out of it. There was a bit of a breeze, and the kite was bobbing around at a great rate, and the streamers were whizzing over the kids' heads. We watched them while we were drying our toes. We didn't have a towel, of course, so we had to use tissues. I do not recommend this: they melt.

'I'd like a kite,' Hal said dreamily, watching the kite soaring overhead.

'Well, I'm sure you could get one,' I said. I am the practical one, in case you haven't noticed. 'I'd say they have them in Spóirt na Mara.' That's the name of the sports shop in the new shopping centre. Very TG4, my father says.

'Oh no,' Hal said. 'I'd have to make it. Otherwise it wouldn't be the same.'

The same as what I never did find out.

After a while we got tired of watching the purple-streaming kite and the kids, and we started to mooch off home. As we got to the edge of the strand – there's a rocky bit just before the sea wall – Hal stooped down and grabbed a handful of beach pebbles and put them in his pocket.

'What are you going to do with those?' I asked him.

'They're for Him. I mean, for his shoes. I need to keep my supply replenished.'

'*What?*' I asked suspiciously.

Have I mentioned that my friend Hal is a bit of a weirdo? Not megaweird, not so's you'd notice on a good day with the wind to his back, but still quite peculiar at times. I could feel one of Hal's weirdnesses coming on with this business of the pebbles.

'Well, you know,' he said, as if it was the most reasonable thing in the world to be discussing, 'if you put a pebble in each shoe every night, then the stock soon runs down.'

'Him', by the way, the one with the shoes, is Hal's sort-of-stepfather. His real name is Alec, but Hal never calls him anything except 'Him'. As you can gather, Hal was not too fond of Alec.

Alec and Hal's mum weren't actually married. I don't know why – most people of that age seem to be – but Hal had this theory that they had something up their sleeves, because Alec had moved in with them only a few weeks before 'on a trial basis', and Hal said that meant they were probably going to get hitched, and he was desperate to make sure that they didn't.

Fat chance of preventing that, if you ask me. Grown-ups have their own ideas when it comes to who they want to marry and there's no point in kids having an opinion, that's for sure, because it'll only End in Tears, as my mum says. (My mum is not bad for an adult, but like all mothers she has these maddening little sayings.)

'You put *pebbles* in Alec's shoes every night?' I imagine you could have heard the surprise in my voice several miles (or knots or fathoms or whatever it is) out to sea.

'Yeah,' said Hal offhandedly, as if everyone did it.

'But that's mean,' I said. 'Also ineffective.'

'What do you mean "ineffective"?'

'Well, Hal, think about it. If you found there were stones in your shoes every single morning, what would you think?'

'I'd think it must be a poor unhappy boy trying to give me the message that I am not welcome in his family.'

'No, you wouldn't, Hal. What you'd think is: somehow or other, for some unfathomable reason, there are pebbles in my shoes every morning; therefore, I should shake out my shoes before I put them on.'

'Oh,' said Hal. 'I never thought of that.'

'So there's no point, is there?' I said.

But I bet he went on doing it anyway.

I asked Hal a few more questions about his home life after that, and it turned out he had a whole one-boy campaign going on to make life difficult for Alec. For example, he used to leave the hot tap running – on *purpose* – to waste the hot water. Also, he opened the windows in cold weather, so that they would have to pay more for the central heating. This took the biscuit for weird behaviour, in my view, as well as being environment-unfriendly in the extreme. Anyway, it was probably his mother who paid the heating bills, since it was her house, but I suppose he wanted to annoy her as well.

'But what about global warming?' I said, when he let me in on this fiendish little secret.

'I don't think the heat escaping from our windows is going to melt any icebergs,' he said loftily.

'It's not icebergs, you dolt,' I said. 'It's the ice *cap*. But that's not the point. The point is that it's terribly wasteful.'

'Exactly,' he said. 'Of their money. That'll teach them.'

'No!' I said in exasperation. 'It's a waste of *oil*, which is a scarce resource, and it means even more fossil fuel is burnt, and that contributes to global warming. That's very irresponsible of you, Hal.'

'Oh!' he said. 'I never thought of that.'

There are a lot of things Hal hasn't ever thought of, you may have noticed.

'Hal, you are so weird,' I said.

And not all that desperately intelligent either, I thought to myself, because if your plan is to make sure your mother doesn't marry someone, putting stones in his shoes is really not terribly likely to work, is it? It might give you some small evil pleasure, sure enough, but as a master plan for influencing the future shape of your family, I'd say it scores about zilch.

'Anyway, I don't understand what is so awful about Alec,' I said.

'It's hard to explain,' Hal said shiftily.

'Well, look, is he mean to you? Does he, you know, hit you, or – em – anything?'

By 'anything' I meant those awful things you read about in the papers that bad adults do to children that make them utterly miserable and mess them up for life. I didn't really want to think about it, but it must be absolutely terrible if that happens to you, so I made a special effort to listen to Hal, in case that was the problem. I was quite pleased with myself for thinking of it.

'No,' Hal said. 'He's not – no, it's not that.'

'So what is it then?'

'He's just – *there*,' Hal said. 'I liked it better before.'

'Hmm,' I said.

'He snores,' Hal added. 'I can hear Him, even through the bedroom door.'

'He snores,' I said. 'That is not exactly a jailing offence, Hal.'

'No, and he – eh, picks his nose. I saw Him once.'

Oh gross, I thought, but I said, 'Everyone picks their nose, Hal. In private. Was he in private?'

'Well, he thought he was, I suppose,' Hal said.

'That doesn't count then,' I said. 'What else?'

'He slurps his tea,' Hal said. 'And he hogs the remote control.'

'Hal, you are just describing a person being a *person*. Everyone hogs the remote if they get a chance. You have to make allowances for other people. That's just – *life*, you know?'

'But he shouldn't be in *my* life,' Hal said fiercely. 'I just don't want Him *around*. It was better when it was just me and my mum.'

'Hal, he's been around for *years*; it's time you got used to it. And if your mum is going to marry him, well, you'll be a proper family then, won't you? And that's nice, isn't it?'

I was trying to look on the bright side, you know, cheer him up, but I think it was just that Alec was not Hal's dad. I'd say that was the problem, nothing to do with Alec himself, not really. I know that is a bit psychological of me, but it stands to reason, doesn't it? You wouldn't want somebody else in your family, would you, that didn't belong there? I wouldn't anyway. I like things staying the way they are, and I bet Hal is the same. And a step-parent is for life, isn't he, not just for Christmas?

Alec was going to have a rough time with Hal. I could see it coming. But I was Hal's friend. I had to take his side, didn't I? No matter what.

Chapter 4

I have two other so-called friends, Rosemarie and Gilda, but they annoy me a lot of the time – there was an incident last term about a jacket that I haven't forgiven them for – so I mostly just hang around with Hal at school. That's not the only reason I am friendly with Hal, of course; I also like him a lot. Hal is like a little white mouse with a twitchy nose. You can't help liking him, even if the twitch drives you mad.

The only other boy I know really well apart from Hal is my older brother, Larry. He is the very opposite of Hal in every way. Larry follows a football team, for example. You can probably guess that Hal doesn't do anything as ordinary as that. I know which team Larry follows, but I'm not going to tell you, because if you have your own favourite team, it might be the same one, and then you would think that Larry must be a great fellow and really like him, and that wouldn't be right at all, because Larry is the world's drippiest drip. He's not evil, but he's dead boring. My mother says it's just the age difference between us that is the problem, and when I am older I will appreciate Larry's excellent qualities, and meanwhile I should give him the benefit of the doubt.

I'll try to give you an example of what Larry is like, so you'll understand my problem.

'If you were a cathedral,' Hal asked me one day, 'would you be Gothic or Romanesque?' (We did cathedrals at school, because our teacher is into cool stuff like that. We have the best teacher ever. She's the nearest adult I can think of to a kid.)

This is a game we call Biscuits, by the way, because it began with a question about biscuits: 'If you were a biscuit, would you be a Kimberley or a Mikado?' The game is that you answer the question and you explain why. For example, I would be a Kimberley – you know, the squidgy ones with the gingery outsides – because there is a bit of spice to me. Rosemarie and Gilda would both be Mikado – pink and fluffy and too sweet to be good for you. It goes on and on: 'If you were a woman in the Bible, would you be Ruth or Naomi?' 'If you were a hero-warrior, would you be Fionn Mac Cumhail or Cú Chulainn?' It's quite a good game if you like that sort of thing, and you find things out about people that you wouldn't have suspected.

'I wouldn't be a cathedral,' Larry butted in. 'I'd rather be the Coliseum.'

Now, that is typical of Larry. Wants to muscle in on me and Hal's games all the time, and messing everything up.

We both turned on him and yelled, because that's cheating, of course. You can't bob out and change the question because if you let people do that, the whole game would just disintegrate and there wouldn't be any point to it. Rosemarie and Gilda would be two semi-detached houses with mown lawns and stiff little hedges, but that wasn't the question asked.

'You can't be the Coliseum,' I said sternly. 'You have to stick with cathedrals. That's how the game works. You answer the question asked.'

'Oh,' said Larry. 'I didn't know that.'

'And anyway, ' I said, 'nobody asked you. I'd be Gothic,' I said then, to Hal, 'and so would you. Larry'd be Romanesque.'

'No, I wouldn't,' said Larry. 'I could be the same as you two. Why do I have to be different?'

Larry doesn't know anything about cathedrals, even though he is older than us. They don't do interesting stuff where he goes to school, only maths and French and economics. But he is definitely Romanesque: symmetrical and straightforward, a bit like a penguin, very black-and-white. Hal and I are Gothic because we're over-the-top with unexpected twists and maybe just a little bit monstrous.

Well, I suppose it wasn't really Larry's fault he didn't understand the game properly, so to be nice to him, I said, 'Let's play "I Spy".'

Now, you probably think of this as a little kids' game, and that is exactly what it is, but Larry likes it, even though he is practically drawing the old-age pension, because he can always think up things that are impossible to guess – words like 'flange' or 'pivot', which no sane person under about thirty-five knows – but you can never say he's cheating because there always is one of those mad things in the room, so he wins.

I don't mind him winning, but it gets boring after a while if you know you are never going to be able to guess the answers, though I have to admit you do get to know a lot of useless words.

After a while I noticed that Hal wasn't joining in the guessing. It was a word beginning with 'h', and I'd tried all the obvious things like house and Hal and hearth and honey and herringbone-patterned curtains. (We don't usually allow adjectives, but I was scraping the barrel.) When I looked at Hal for inspiration he was muttering something to himself.

'Is that a spell you're chanting?' I asked him.

'Hmm,' he said.

'Hmm?' I guessed, though of course you can't spy a hmm. (I told you, I was scraping the barrel.)

Larry shook his head and looked smug.

'It's my plan,' said Hal. 'I'm working out the details.'

'Plan doesn't begin with "h",' I said, which was a very feeble joke, but I was tired of the game by now.

'No. I mean I'm just hatching it,' Hal said.

'Hatch?' I guessed. We were in our dining room and there is a hatch into the kitchen. We don't use it, because there's a computer in front of it, so it's barely visible, which is why I hadn't guessed it before.

'There, you see!' said Larry crossly. 'That's what happens when I choose an ordinary word – you win. I should have stuck with my first idea, which was "hasp".'

'Is there a hasp?' I asked, looking around. I was not exactly sure what a hasp was, but I had an idea it had something to do with windows.

'No,' said Larry. 'That's why I had to change it to hatch.'

This was such a ridiculous thing that we all collapsed in giggles and for the next quarter of an hour all we could think of to say to each other was, 'Well, of course, "hasp" is a much more difficult word to guess; the only problem is there isn't a hasp in the house,' and then we'd go off into gales of laughter again. 'There isn't a hasp in the house,' we'd roar, 'not a one.'

But Hal was not to be distracted, and after a

while he said to Larry, 'We need you for this plan.'

Note that fatal 'we'. That included me, I could feel it in my bones, but I hadn't agreed to anything. I rolled my eyes. I couldn't imagine what was coming next, but I knew it wouldn't be good.

'We need someone with a grown-up voice to leave a message on his answering machine,' Hal explained.

There he went with that 'we' again. Anyway, I wouldn't exactly say that Larry's voice is grown-up. It's sort of baritonish, I suppose, most of the time, but it's still at that stage where it could go off the scale at any moment. All the same, I suppose it is more grown-up than Hal's pipsqueaky little treble.

'No,' I said sharply. 'Leave Larry out of this, Hal. Whatever it is.'

I could just see Hal landing us all in some sort of trouble, and I'd end up, as usual, being the one having to do all the explaining, and if Larry was in on whatever it was from the outset, then he'd know everything, whatever there was to know, and I'd have a hard time trying to explain it all away with him hovering about saying, 'It was all Olivia's fault,' which is probably his favourite sentence in the world.

Hal gave me a pained look. It's hard to describe a pained look but you'll know it if you ever see it. It's where a person looks at you as if you have said or done the most incredibly insensitive thing and deeply hurt their feelings, but they are not going to say anything because they are such a fine person, and then you feel really small and you would do anything to prove to them that really you love them to bits and you wouldn't dream of hurting them.

'Larry won't mind helping out,' Hal said. 'And it's nothing to worry about; it's just a little practical joke really.'

'We don't do practical jokes, Hal,' I said. 'That's not our style.'

That's not exactly what I meant. What I meant was that anything Hal was going to come up with was probably going to be seriously cookie. I mean, think of the cookiest idea you can imagine and then double its cookie value, and that's the kind of cookie idea Hal has.

'Olivia, I need to get this man out of my life,' he said. 'Are you going to help me or not?'

Now, I know that sounds as if he was going to *murder* someone, but I knew Hal wouldn't really do anything totally evil. I was kind of curious to know what exactly he had in mind. And anyway, distracting him from leaving hot taps running just to spite his sort-of-stepfather was quite a useful thing and could be my good deed for the environment this summer, so I caved in and said, 'Go on then, tell us.'

'Well,' said Hal, 'this is the plan, but you have

to promise Utter Secrecy before I tell you. You must not breathe a word about my plan, especially not to anyone old enough to vote, or I won't let you in on it. Promise? Cross your hearts and hope to die?'

You know, if he hadn't made it all sound so mysterious, we'd probably have lost interest in the whole project, and then it might never have happened, but he'd got me hooked now, so I nodded. I crossed my heart and turned my palm outwards and vowed eternal secrecy.

This was a bad, bad move. And the worst part is, I knew it, even at the time, but that doesn't always help, does it? You can know something is all wrong and still you find yourself getting dragged into it, because the other person is so set on it.

Oh dear.

If this was a film instead of a book, there'd be eerie music with an insistent drumbeat in the background at this point: dooh-dooh-DOOH-dooh, dooh-dooh-DOOH-dooh, ka-bim, ka-bam, ka-BOOM.

You can probably guess that All Did Not Go According to Plan.

Chapter 5

I bet you've been wondering when I am going to get back to the kite. I didn't know you were so interested in kites. Maybe you weren't, but now you are because I have made it sound interesting. I hope so.

Well, the day after that conversation about the Great Secret Plan, I went over to Hal's house and I found him in that chilly garage again, surrounded by kite-making equipment, although the kite was pretty well finished. It was recognizably a kite, I mean, but he hadn't painted it yet, and it looked quite dull, like an egg box, no particular colour, just generally pale.

Hal was mixing paints with an air of great concentration. I was glad to see him doing something constructive and fairly ordinary. Maybe he'd forget about his cookie plan and go back to kites. That'd be a relief all round.

'I have to get the right shade of blue,' he muttered, when I asked him what he was doing.

'Why?' I said. 'Does it matter?' I'd given up on trying to persuade him to use a more sensible colour. 'Most shades of blue are nice.' (There's that word again. It's much more useful than teachers ever let on.)

'It has to be Friday blue,' he explained.

'Why?' I asked.

'Because,' said Hal.

'Well, that clears *that* up,' I said witheringly, but Hal doesn't really notice if you wither him.

I was kind of curious to find out what shade of blue Fridays are if you're Hal, so I didn't ask any more questions, just watched.

He dibbed and dabbed with blues and blacks and whites for a good while. He even put a tiny streak of red into the mixture. I was sure that was going to ruin it, but it didn't. It seemed to make it go even bluer, if you can imagine that happening.

'That's it,' he said at last, after he'd stirred in a big glob of white. 'That's blue like Friday.' He sat back with a big cheesy grin on his face, as if he'd won the marathon or something.

'It's blue like the sky,' I said.

It really was and it was gorgeous. It was blue like the sky, china blue. It was a shade of blue to make your heart sing. It was so clear and blue a blue, you couldn't imagine ever thinking of anything else as blue.

He shrugged.

The paints smelt good. When my mum or dad paints at home it usually smells disgusting and makes your chest ache. But there was a warm smell to this paint of Hal's. I said so, and Hal squinched up his eyes and looked hard at me.

'Good,' he said. 'You're getting there.'

I had no idea what he meant, which made a change, because it's usually the other way round.

He painted the kite blue all over so that it was like this wonderful giant blue butterfly with its wings spread out. When it was dry we took it to the strand for its maiden voyage.

When I was a little girl, my parents took me to see a picture. Not a film, a painting. (My parents are like that. Other people's parents take them to Disneyland. Oh well, lah-dee-dah.) I don't know where it was, or what the picture was called or anything, but I do remember the picture itself. It showed a lot of people doing pleasant Sunday afternoon things and wearing their Sunday best, old-fashioned clothes, long dresses and suits with high collars. I don't remember any of them flying a kite, but when I thought of kite-flying, I always thought of that picture. I imagined a lot of people standing about sedately, with a kite bobbing politely up above their heads, and everyone would be admiring it and giving delighted little grins at each other, and occasionally giving the kite string a little tug in this direction or that.

But it wasn't a bit like that. Usually, we cycle to the strand, but we had to walk this time because of the kite, which was too big to carry on a bike. There was quite a stiff little breeze as we left Hal's house, and by the time we got to the strand it had started to get a lot blowier. I mean, windy to the point where you couldn't be sure your clothes were going to stay on unless you buttoned everything up very tightly, so we did, because it would be a bit embarrassing if our clothes were all whipped off.

'That's great,' Hal shouted to me. 'The kite will really take off in this wind.'

Well, it did that all right.

I don't know how Hal managed to get it up into the air. He sort of hurled it away from his body several times, and it just flapped wildly for a bit and landed more or less at his feet, like a dejected dog. Then it would take off again for a few metres, but then it straggled to the sand again, where it blew and blustered and looked like a large piece of blue litter. But then he did something different, gave a twist with his wrist or something as he launched it, and suddenly it was off – and off, and off, and Hal was trotting and leaping after it, his anorak fluttering and waving as he ran.

The kite was like some sort of wild creature, tossing and lurching angrily through the air and wrenching him along with it. He's not big, Hal, though he's wiry and plenty strong, I'd have thought, but it was as if a ragdoll was taking a very large and bouncy dog for a walk, the kind of dog that is always jumping into bins and sniffing up lady dogs and making loud and enthusiastic snuffling sounds and whining with excitement and skittering along with all four paws going in different directions.

So there Hal was, dancing about at the end of the kite string, being pulled along like a feather duster tied to the back of a juggernaut breaking the speed limit. I began to imagine that he might get yanked out over the water, and I didn't think he'd go floating off merrily like Mary Poppins, waving a stately goodbye; no, there'd come a sudden gust and a flurry and he'd be whisked out to sea, and then there'd be a crash-landing on an inconveniently placed rock and it'd be goodbye for keeps, Hal, it's been nice knowing you, weird boy.

'Oi, oi! You kids, oi!' came this voice over the wind, which was whipping my hair around my face at this stage.

You read about people shouting 'oi', don't you, but I'd never heard anybody actually yelling it in real life. It was like a bad mobile phone connection, because of the way the wind whisked bits of the sound off in different directions, but we got the message all the same.

We spun round. Well, I spun round. I don't know

about Hal; he was probably spinning anyway, at the end of the kite string.

The owner of the voice was this enormously fat man, like Tweedledee and Tweedledum and Billy Bunter rolled into one, with the tiniest little dog you ever saw yapping along at his feet. He wasn't wobbly fat, the Tweedle character. He was just a walking mountain. His feet were quite small. I couldn't imagine how his ankles didn't buckle under the weight of his body. Also, I wondered where he found clothes to fit him. If you took his belt off and laid it out along the ground, it'd reach from here to Limerick. No, that's an exaggeration, and I am trying to break my exaggeration habit. From my house to Hal's house then.

'Oi!' he yelled again, and he was beckoning towards us with an arm as big as a branch. His voice sounded English, though it was hard to tell from a single syllable.

There was something irresistible about this huge person in unbelievably enormous trousers with his teeny little dog frisking about his ankles, so I went and stood in front of Tweedledeedumbunter and said 'Yes?' with as much dignity as I could muster, considering most of my hair was in my mouth.

The little dog started to lick my toes excitedly, with his hot, damp tongue. It was quite nice for just about a second, but then it got cold almost immediately. I wondered if my skin tasted salty.

Tweedledeedumbunter looked down at me and shouted, 'Will you tell your foolish young friend there to bring down that kite at once, like a good girl? This is no weather for kiting. Look sharp now, chop-chop, no time to lose; we don't want to be fishing him out of the sea, do we?'

He was English all right, but not like a real English person that you might see on the telly having a beer and telling a joke, more like a person out of one of those musty old books Larry used to read when he was my age that he got from my dad, who also used to read them when he was my age. I read one or two of them myself, and they are not too bad, though they are mainly for boys and have more shipwrecks in them than you'd really want to read about.

He was right, Mr TD Bunter. We did not want to be fishing Hal out of the sea, and I was kind of relieved that a grown-up person was being bossy about it.

I turned my head and looked at Hal, who was still racing along in pursuit of the kite.

'I don't think he can,' I said to TDB. 'I think it's out of control.'

He sighed a great fat sigh and then he lumbered steadily towards Hal, and I trotted along after him.

Hal had stopped running. He seemed to have worked out that running after the kite was only encouraging it, so now he was standing still and hanging on for dear life. When Tweedledeedum-bunter got to within a metre or two of Hal he boomed out, 'May I?'; and at the same time he reached over Hal's shoulder towards the kite.

Hal was still hanging on to the bobbin, or whatever you call the thing you wind the string around, but he stepped back to make space (a lot of space) for TDB, who caught hold of the kite string rather awkwardly between his huge flat thumb and his equally huge index finger, like an elephant getting hold of a lollipop. The kite bucked and tossed like a mad bird over his head, but he just stood placidly watching it for a moment, like a great, thoughtful human anchor. After a minute or two, he signalled to Hal to pass him the bobbin, and then, slowly, unconcernedly, as if he was landing a small and unchallenging sprat, he wound in the line and brought the kite down.

'Eh, thanks,' muttered Hal, half resentful and half grateful. His face was bright red and streaming with perspiration, and his chest was heaving with the effort of controlling the mad kite.

'My pleasure,' said the large gentleman with a small inclination of his head, and I declare to goodness, it was almost a bow. 'Now, my advice to you young'uns is to fly this kite in a brisk breeze – a breeze, mind, not a storm-force wind. You never fly a kite in a small hurricane, if you want to keep it.'

It wasn't a small hurricane – that was an exaggeration and he threw in the 'small' so you'd be distracted into thinking he was being accurate – it was just a bit on the stormy side.

'Eh, thanks,' said Hal again.

'Rightio then,' said Tweedledeedumbunter. "And by the way, your kite needs a tail. Helps to stabilize it, you know. Cut along home now, both of you, and don't talk to any more strangers.'

We had, of course, completely forgotten we weren't supposed to talk to strangers, and this one definitely qualified as strange. I slapped my hand across my mouth to keep from laughing, but I could see he knew I was sniggering – I couldn't help it: it was the way he talked. He shook his head gravely, as if he was disappointed in me, but he bowed almost imperceptibly again, and then he whistled to his dog (though the dog was right there at his feet all the time) and continued on calmly with his walk.

We watched his back view as he sailed along like a giant iceberg in men's clothes. The wind flapped frantically at the edges of his jacket, and his tie flew out first on one side and then on the other, but he just ploughed implacably forward. After a few moments, as a particularly nasty squall of wind blew up, he bent down and picked up the little dog and tucked him in between his elbow and his body, and on he continued until he was out of sight.

'That was a close one,' I said to Hal as we walked off.

'Yeah, I was afraid it might disintegrate up there,' he said.

'It wasn't the *kite* I was worried about,' I said. 'It was you.'

Hal stopped walking and looked at me. 'Me?' he said incredulously. 'Why me?'

'Because you were on the end of the string,' I said. 'You were going to be yanked out to sea at any minute.'

'No, I wasn't,' said Hal. 'I hadn't a notion of it.'

'You didn't need to have a notion of it,' I said. 'It was the wind that had the notions.'

'Not at all,' said Hal, but he had a secret little grin on his face. I think he was pleased that I'd been worried about him.

He is a daft old thing.

Chapter 6

Hal had not forgotten about his life-changing plan. This was the deal, right: Larry was to leave a message on Alec's voicemail after office hours on Friday evening. Hal had written the whole thing out.

One thing you need to know, by the way, is that Alec is a painter. Not an artist – a housepainter. My dad says he makes loads of money at it, but people always think that about other people's jobs, don't they? Anyway, that's what he does, and he has a little white van and overalls that are all multicoloured from the different paints he's spilt on them over the years.

This is how the message went, the one Larry was supposed to leave on Alec's mobile:

> Hello, Mr Denham, Balnamara General here, Clem Callaghan, maintenance manager. We have a painting job, bit of a rush on it; we need you here first thing in the morning, double

rates, no, sorry, *triple* rates because of the bank holiday weekend. Now, this is where you have to go . . .

Then came directions about what he was to do when he arrived at the hospital. Something about turning right past the physiotherapy department and a long, low building with a green door, and then something about how the paint would be there, no need to bring any.

That was it. That was the master plan that Hal was so proud of. He was going to get Alec to paint a long, low building behind the physiotherapy department at the local hospital. Well, big deal! That was really going to get Alec out of his life, right?

I don't think so.

'I'm not doing it,' Larry said flatly, when he saw the speech.

For once I could see his point of view. This was the weirdest thing that weird-boy Hal had come up with in living memory.

'Clem Callaghan,' I said. 'What a name! Did you make it up, Hal?'

'No,' said Hal, 'I got it in the phone book.'

'Hal, if you've stolen someone's name out of the phone book, that means they are real and they might sue you or something.'

'No, it's not a real name.'

'You just *said* you got it in the phone book. They only have real names in the phone book, Hal.'

Hal threw his eyes up. 'You use a pin,' he said.

'Yes?' I said.

'You close your eyes and stick the pin in.'

'And you get a *real name*,' I said.

'No,' said Hal, 'you get a real surname. Then you do it again, on a different page, and you get a first name. Then you put them together and you have a new name. It doesn't belong to anyone.'

'Oh!' I said.

'Cool, isn't it?' he said.

'Yeah, brilliant,' I said sarcastically.

Hal ignored me. He turned to Larry.

'Larry, please,' he said. 'You *have* to do it. *Please*.'

'I don't have to,' said Larry. 'You can't make me and it's a stupid idea.'

'But, Larry, you're the only one with a grown-up voice.'

Larry smirked.

'And you're such a good actor,' Hal said.

Which is total rubbish. Larry smirked some more.

'Look, Hal,' Larry said and there was a swagger in his voice, as if he was a very wise old person talking to a very silly young person, 'there's a flaw in this plan of yours.'

Hal made his eyes go wide, as if he was ever so

grateful to Larry for taking the trouble to point this out to him.

'What's that, Larry?' he asked humbly.

'Well, in the first place, how do you know Alec won't just *answer the phone*? Then I wouldn't get to leave the message. I'd have to talk to him and he'd be sure to ask an awkward question that I couldn't answer, and then the whole thing would just collapse.'

'I can see that you might be concerned, Larry,' said Hal. 'But you see, the thing is, he always turns his mobile off when he comes home; my mother doesn't want people ringing Him in the evenings. It'll switch to voicemail when you phone Him. And he does check his voicemails: he has a business to run.'

'Hmm,' said Larry. 'But he'll try to ring this Clegg person back, won't he?'

'Clem,' said Hal. 'But here's the thing. We're going to make the phone call from a public phone box. There's one in the Market Square, opposite the post office. It's working, I checked. So it won't matter if he does try to phone back. Nobody will answer it. He won't be able to get hold of Clem. He's probably gone out anyway. It's Friday night, remember.'

'Who?'

'Clem!'

'Clem doesn't exist, Hal.'

'Well then!' said Hal, as if he'd just proved a point.

I didn't think it was much of a plan, and I could see that Larry wasn't impressed either. Even if we could make it work, what was the point? So what if we got Alec to paint a long, low building with a green door? That was hardly going to change the world, was it? It certainly wasn't going to have any effect on Hal's mum's and Alec's wedding plans.

Can you just imagine it? 'Oh, you painted that building on Saturday, the long, low one. I don't think we can be married after all. Sorry.'

'Hal,' I said, 'what exactly is the point here?'

'The point is,' said Hal, 'that if Alec is out painting this . . . this place on Saturday morning, then he can't take my mother down the country to her golf tournament, can he?'

'Your mother is going to a golf tournament?'

'Not just going to it. She is *playing* in it! She has been looking forward to it for weeks.'

'And you don't want her to play in it?' I asked. 'Is that it?'

I always think golf is like hurling standing still. I can never understand why people want to play it. But then I'm not a grown-up. They're different.

'No, that's not it,' said Hal, 'not exactly. The thing is, they have a date for it, my mother and Him.'

'A date? They *live* together, Hal. People who live together don't go on *dates*.'

'That's the problem,' Hal explained. 'He never takes her out, my mum says. And she's always moaning that he doesn't take her golf seriously, so this time he's promised *faithfully* to go with her and she's all excited about it; she's even bought a special outfit and everything. But now, if he gets this important job with all that extra money . . . he won't go with her and she'll be furious. There'll be a big row. She might even *kick Him out*.'

His eyes were shining at the thought of it.

You think this is a fairly feeble plan, right? I do too, but at the time it did seem to make some sort of weird sense. Hal can be quite convincing when he's all worked up about something. And he really was worked up about this.

'So let's imagine that Larry leaves this message on Alec's phone,' I said. 'Then what?'

'Then he will take the job, and the next morning early, *we* are going to follow Him, to see how it all works out,' Hal said.

'Not me,' said Larry quickly. 'I have a plane to catch on Saturday morning. School trip to Paris.'

'Not to worry,' said Hal. 'Just me and Olivia will be plenty. You go to Paris, Lar; we can handle the rest.'

I don't think Larry knew what hit him. Somehow, it seemed, he was going to make this crazy phone call, even though he'd never actually agreed to do it. I suppose he could have put his foot down, but Hal had somehow bamboozled him, blinded him with the brilliance of it all or something, I don't know.

'Me?' I squeaked. '*Follow* him! Oh, Hal, I don't like this. This is a weirdness too far for me.'

'But, Olivia, I'm – desperate,' Hal said.

'You're desperate all right,' I muttered. I don't think he heard me. 'Why, Hal?' I said aloud. 'Why is it so important?'

'She's . . . they're . . .'

'What, Hal?'

'Boarding school,' he said. 'She said if I don't start getting on with Him, I'll have to go to boarding school. She says I make her life a misery and she can't stand it any longer.'

Boarding school. Well, that mightn't be too bad. There might be making apple-pie beds and having midnight feasts and putting whoopee cushions on the teachers' chairs and that sort of thing. It might be quite fun.

But I didn't say any of that to Hal. I just asked, 'Well, *do* you, you know – make her life a misery? Apart from leaving the taps running and so on.'

'No.'

'So what's her problem then? Why is she going to send you to boarding school?'

'Well, I suppose it's because I don't talk to Him.'

‘Oh, Hal!’

‘I wish you wouldn’t always say “Oh, Hal!”, Olivia.’

‘Sorry, but you mean, you don’t talk to him *at all?* As in, not a word? As in, “Will you ask him to pass me the sugar”?’

‘Yeah, pretty much.’

‘And you haven’t spoken to him for *two years*?’

‘No!’ said Hal. ‘I mean, I used to talk to Him. I used to say, oh hello and well goodbye, and that kind of thing. But since he moved in with us – well, you can’t always be saying hello to someone if they *live* there, can you? It’s not like they are a guest any more.’

‘So you say nothing at all?’

‘Yeah,’ said Hal. ‘I mean, he shouldn’t really be there, should he? So I pretend he’s not.’

I couldn’t think of an argument against that. It made a sort of Hal-ish sense.

‘And now they’ve started threatening you with boarding school?’

‘Well, it’s mainly her. I don’t think he really minds much. But she does. She’s been on about it for ages, but now we’re coming to the end of primary school, so it’s getting a bit more urgent. She has *brochures* for places where they make you play rugby.’

I looked at Hal and tried to imagine him in rugby gear. It didn’t work. He kept disappearing up his own sleeves.

'OK, Hal,' I said with a sigh. 'I think this is a daft plan, but if you really feel you need to take a stand, well, I'll go with you. But I'm only going to make sure you don't get into trouble, OK?'

Ah me, doomed words.

Chapter 7

Saturday morning came. I could have had a nice lie-in, but no; instead, I got up early and bicycled over to Hal's house *before breakfast.* There'd been a small change of plan. It seems we would never be able to follow Alec in his van, so now, instead of that, we were going to cycle *ahead* of him to the hospital and wait there to see what happened. I really didn't see the point of all this, but Hal insisted.

Normally, I couldn't have got away with leaving the house at the crack of dawn, I'd have been missed at home, only they were all fussing about getting Larry to the airport in time for his flight and giving him long and complex instructions about how he was to behave himself when he got to Paris and how he was to have absolutely NO alcohol of any description, no way, no, no, no.

Larry doesn't drink. Let's face it, Larry is not one of nature's rebels.

But my parents don't believe this. They believe all that stuff they read in the papers about Teenage

Drinking. Larry is not exactly what you would call a typical teenager. I probably will be, when I get to that age. I will most likely be a total handful, get studs everywhere, wear the most way-out things, listen to really objectionable music. I will drive my parents up the wall. They've had it easy with Larry. They won't know what hit them. I am looking forward to it.

I got a list of instructions too, of course, before they left for the airport, about how I wasn't to open the door to strangers and I wasn't to light any fires or leave the cooker turned on and how they'd be right back as soon as Larry's plane boarded. I waved them off at the front door, and as soon as they'd left, I leapt on to my bike and scooted over to Hal's.

My cookie friend, I said to myself as I rode out of our estate, along the main road, past the Centra shop, round the corner into Hal's estate, past all the nice calm-looking gardens with their flower beds and their little gates with notices about Beware of the Dog and their Welcome mats on the doorsteps and wishing wells in the middle of the lawns – all those houses with their curtains closed and sensible people inside them in their beds, which is where I should have been. My weird friend. Rosemarie and Gilda were beginning to look much more acceptable. At least they wouldn't have me up at the crack of dawn bicycling around town on a mad escapade like this. They wouldn't have the imagination for it to start with.

Hal was waiting for me at his gate, looking pale and anxious, with his bike.

Alec's painter's van stood in the driveway, a little white van with a ladder on the roof rack and 'ALEXANDER DENHAM INTERIOR AND EXTERIOR PAINTWORK NO JOB TOO SMALL' painted on the side of it in rainbow colours, like the writing on a Noddy book.

'Hi, Hal!' I called.

Hal made a zipping signal across his mouth to shut me up, and he indicated that I was to dismount.

'What's wrong?' I asked in a loud whisper.

'Nothing,' he whispered back. 'But he's up already; we haven't much of a headstart, so we have to dash, OK?'

I nodded.

'Right,' said Hal throatily, 'wheel your bike *quietly* to the end of the road and then we'll cycle from there.'

I nodded again. I am so cooperative really. And away we went. Against my better judgement.

There wasn't much traffic about early on a Saturday morning, so we made good headway by cycling like mad. Every time a car came up behind us Hal turned round to check if it was Alec, but it never was.

'Maybe he's not going to do it,' I yelled at Hal when we stopped at the traffic lights in town. 'Maybe he doesn't want to. Maybe your mother has made him go to the golf with her after all. Who's supposed to be minding you, by the way?'

'I mind myself,' Hal said.

'You don't!'

'Yeah, I do. Unless it's night-time. Come on, Olivia,' he suddenly yelled, spurting ahead as the lights changed to green. 'Keep up!'

I jumped on to my pedals and I kept churning all the way over to the hospital. We got off at the gate and I hung over my handlebars, trying to get my breath back after our crazy bike ride.

The hospital is a big sprawling place with blue railings and a lot of low, flat-roofed buildings. Just inside the gate, on the left, is a large noticeboard with signs in different colours that point you to the various departments, and on the right, before the noticeboard, is a glass kiosk sort of thing, with a security man in it. There's a red-and-orange striped pole that goes across the gate, so you can't get in unless the security man raises it.

As soon as I could talk, I said, 'Well, are you sure he got the message?'

Hal was pretty winded too. 'I think he must've,' he gasped. He breathed a bit and then he went on. 'There was an ALMIGHTY row this morning. My mother threw her shoes out the window.'

'Why?' I wondered if maybe Hal had put stones in her shoes as well.

'I have no idea. Anyway, she came down in her bare feet and her new outfit and she jumped into her car and zoomed off to her golf tournament without even having any breakfast.'

This house was beginning to sound odder and odder. I mean, it's one thing to start turning a garage into a playroom and then go off the idea. It's another thing to start threatening an odd little squirt like Hal with six years of compulsory rugby and another thing again to throw your shoes out the window because someone won't take you to a game of golf. Maybe they were always flinging things out of the window. Maybe they did worse than that.

'Oh, Hal,' I said.

'So you see, Olivia?'

I did kind of see. His family certainly seemed a bit peculiar, I have to say. I started to feel a bit sorry for Hal, and there's only one of him too, which makes it harder. Larry would not be my idea of a person to spend the rest of my life on a desert island with, but if the chips were down, we'd stick together, me and Lar. Poor old Hal had no one. Only me.

'But, Hal, you know, you can't mess with grown-ups. They always win in the end.'

Hal shrugged.

We were just locking our bikes to a railing, out of sight behind a parked car on the other side of the road from the hospital gate, when Alec's little white van appeared at the end of the road, and there was Alec hunched over the steering wheel, looking right and left before turning into the road we were on.

To be fair to Hal, Alec wouldn't exactly be my idea of someone I'd like to meet at breakfast every day from now until I was old enough to leave home. He's a bit – ferrety. And his face is shiny. I don't know what it is about shiny faces, but they give me the creeps.

I'm sorry if you have a shiny face and you are reading this. You are probably a lovely person, and you most likely have compensating features, such as not being ferrety. Having an aversion to shiny faces probably says more about me than it does about the person with the shiny face, but anyway, Alec is a man with a shiny face; there is no getting away from it.

We crouched down behind the parked cars and watched. It should have been adventurous, but I just felt a bit light-headed from cycling all that way with no breakfast and a bit panicky too about what was going to happen next.

Alec drove right up to the orange barrier. We could see him pointing and gesticulating and the security man scratching his head, but eventually the red-and-orange pole went up and the little white van drove in. It stopped at the big notice and then it turned right, in the direction of the physiotherapy department.

'You know, Hal,' I said, watching the little white van disappearing round a building. 'I can't see this all ending in divorce, somehow.'

'They're not married,' Hal said, 'so they can't be divorced.'

'No, but it doesn't matter what you call it. The thing is, Hal, kids can't make adults break up. This isn't going to work. And it'll be boarding school for you in September if you don't start talking to him.'

Hal didn't answer. He just crossed the road to the hospital entrance and took a look around. I trailed along after him, still trying to reason with him, but he wasn't listening.

There was a separate little gate for pedestrians. We could just saunter in without having to go near the security man, if we left the bikes outside. But it was about six hours until visiting time. If we met someone who wanted to know our business, I didn't know how we were going to explain what we were doing wandering around the hospital grounds at this hour of the day.

'Maybe we should just wait here for a while,' I said. 'It won't take him long to discover it's all been a hoax, and then he'll just have to turn round and come out again. Then we can go home.'

'Yeah, OK,' said Hal. He sounded a bit deflated.

We sat on the hospital wall and kicked our heels against it. It was a low brick wall, with prickly things growing behind it, but if you sat carefully you could avoid getting scratched.

My tummy was rumbling.

'I could murder a doughnut,' I said after a while.

'Stop,' said Hal. 'You're making it worse by talking about food.'

Time ticked on.

'The kind with jam in the middle are my favourite,' I said. 'Though I like the ring ones if they have icing on them. And hundreds and thousands.'

'Olivia! Shut it!'

'Half a dozen doughnuts,' I said after a while. 'A *mountain* of doughnuts. I'm starving.'

'Stop!' said Hal. His tummy was rumbling too. I could hear it.

I checked my watch. 'Hal,' I said, 'it's nearly ten o'clock.'

'Yes,' he said, 'long past breakfast-time. That's why we're so hungry.'

'That's not what I mean,' I said. 'I mean, he's been in there a good quarter of an hour. What do you think is going on?'

'Heh-heh,' said Hal.

'Hal?' I said. 'Hal, that building you described behind the physiotherapy department. The one he is supposed to paint. What exactly is it?'

'It's the mortuary,' Hal said. 'Heh-heh!'

'*What?*'

'The mortuary.'

'Hal, is that something like a morgue?'

'Yeah,' said Hal. 'I suppose you could say that. Only smaller.'

'Hal! You can't have!'

'Heh-heh,' said Hal again, sounding like the evil vampire character in a horror movie. 'Heh-heh!'

'Why on earth did you direct him to the morgue, Hal?'

'Well, I was trying to think of the most lugubrious place. It seemed like a good idea.'

'Lugubrious!' I snorted. 'Hal, you are seriously deranged. I mean, I always knew you were weird, but this is positively *Gothic*!'

'Yeah,' he said with a grin. 'You and me, we're Gothic. Like the cathedrals. Aren't we, Olivia?'

I suddenly didn't want to be Gothic any more. I mean, I was on Hal's side, but Romanesque looked quite attractive from where I was sitting, outside that hospital with madboy beside me and my stomach screaming for food. My parents would be home from the airport soon too, and I would be in right trouble if they arrived back to an empty house.

I clenched my teeth and said nothing for what seemed about ten minutes. I checked my watch. Two minutes had passed. It was now exactly ten o'clock. Still no sign of Alec coming back and looking thunderous or puzzled or whatever it was that Hal was hoping for.

'Maybe he got lost,' Hal said after a while. He was starting to get a bit jittery. I could see.

'I'm so hungry,' I said a minute or two later.

'Well, what do you think?' asked Hal. 'Will we go off and get some food someplace, or will we hang on here a bit longer or what?'

I wasn't sure what we were doing there anyway, and I was very tempted by the idea of food, but at the same time I felt we couldn't just walk off and leave poor old Alec in there – with the *bodies*. Even if he did make people throw their shoes out the window. (I suppose she must have been throwing them *at* him. What a pair they must be!)

'Maybe we should go in after him and see what's happened,' I said. 'What do you think, Hal? We got him into this, whatever it is. We are sort of, you know, *responsible*. He might have run into some sort of trouble in there, trying to convince people there is a Clem Clapham on the staff. They might have decided he's an escaped loony or a spy or *anything*.'

'A spy!' snorted Hal. 'What would a spy be doing snooping around a hospital mortuary dressed up like a painter? And it's Callaghan.'

'Well, what would *anyone* be doing snooping around a hospital mortuary?' I said.

'Do you want to wait a bit, so?' Hal asked. He

looked a bit worried himself, though he wouldn't admit it.

'We'll give it another fifteen minutes, will we?' I said.

'OK,' he said. 'And then what?'

I couldn't imagine what we'd do if Alec didn't reappear soon, so I pretended I hadn't heard the question.

Chapter 8

Five minutes crawled by.

'My stomach thinks my throat is cut,' Hal remarked.

'Mine too,' I muttered.

He has to come out soon, I thought. I mean, what can he be doing in there? He must have discovered by now that there is no paint, there is no Clem Callaghan, there is no painting job, there are no triple rates, and he should have gone with his wife – or his not-wife – to the golf tournament and saved himself a heap of trouble.

'Olivia,' Hal said after another little while, 'I don't think he's coming out.'

'He has to come out sometime,' I said. 'We said we'd give it fifteen minutes.'

'OK,' he said with a sigh and kicked the wall some more.

I checked my watch again. Eight minutes past ten.

I began to hallucinate about food. I could see

mounds of mash and great big troughs of porridge and a whole gingerbread house, just waiting to be gobbled and chomped and munched and swallowed.

Time moved agonizingly slowly.

'It's fifteen minutes, Hal,' I said at last, watching the second hand slipping round towards twelve. 'When the second hand hits twelve, it's fifteen minutes from when we said we'd give it fifteen minutes. And that was after he'd already been gone about fifteen minutes. That's half an hour that he's been in there with those dead bodies, Hal.'

'Don't!' said Hal.

'Well, the mortuary part was your idea. In fact, this whole thing was your idea, Hal King. I am suffering from sleep deprivation and I am on the verge of starvation and you expect me to mince my words.'

'Don't say "mince",' wailed Hal.

'Mince!' I said spitefully. 'Hamburger. Bolognese. Mince pies.'

'I can't think if you keep talking about food.'

'And I can't think if I don't eat. If we don't eat soon,' I said, 'there'll be two more candidates for the mortuary.'

'Olivia, that is not nice,' Hal said reproachfully.

'Tell you what,' I said, 'why don't we just ask the security man what the story is? And then we can decide what to do.'

You know, it was a bit weird. There was Hal, trying to get rid of Alec, and now that he had finally disappeared, we were putting all this energy into trying to find him again. Life is not very logical, is it?

Anyway, I went up to the little glass kiosk and knocked.

The security man looked up from his copy of the *Irish Independent.* 'Yes?' he said, opening a little sliding-glass door in the side of the kiosk.

'Did a man drive in here about half an hour ago?' I asked.

'Listen, a-lanna,' said the security man, pushing his peaked hat back off his forehead, 'any number of men have driven in here in the last half hour. Which per-tick-ler man would you be thinking of?'

'The one in the white van with the ladder on top,' I said.

'The painter?' said the security man and laughed. 'Looking for the mortuary? Only he didn't seem to know it *was* the mortuary.'

'That's the one,' I said.

'Ah, yes,' said the security man. 'Yes, indeed.'

'Well?' I said.

'Well, what?'

'Well, where is he now? I mean, would you have any idea?'

'I beg your parsnips?' said the security man.

Parsnips! What was he on about?

'The painter,' I said, enunciating carefully. 'What happened to him?'

'How would I know?'

I looked at Hal. Hal shrugged.

'Is he your da or what?' asked the security man.

'He's *his* da,' I said, pointing at Hal.

Hal opened his mouth in a big 'O' shape, like a goldfish. Please, Hal, I breathed silently. Please don't announce he is not your father, not even your stepfather, he is just this fly-by-night your mother has given houseroom to. Just – don't – say – it. I don't know if thought transference works, but Hal closed his mouth again and said nothing.

'And Saturday is pocket-money day, I suppose,' the man went on, turning it into a joke. 'But I'm afraid I can't help you. I definitely saw him coming in, and a right story he had too, I can tell you, but what I can't tell you is what happened to him once he got inside. I haven't got a telescope in here, you know.' He gave a little chuckle at his own wit and he slid the window closed.

We stood there for a moment. I was wondering what to do next and Hal was blowing his nose. Next thing the little sliding door opened again.

'You two planning on standing there all morning?' the security man asked.

'We were just wondering,' I said carefully, 'suppose he couldn't find who he was looking for in there, what would happen to him?'

'Happen to him?' said the security man. 'Nothing would happen to him. I suppose he'd just come out again, wouldn't he? We haven't got a policy on checking what happens to people who drive in here, you know. We have trouble enough making sure the *patients* get looked after.' He gave a short bark of laughter at that.

'So he's still inside then?' I ventured.

'Well now,' said the security man and he pushed his hat further back off his forehead. It looked as if it might topple over the top of his head and down his back. 'I can't really comment on that. He could be. And then again . . .'

Hal winced.

'And if we went in to look for him . . . ?' I asked tentatively.

'It's a free country,' said the security man, 'and this is a public hospital. As long as you don't go trampling on the flower beds or charging around the wards spreading germs and upsetting people, you're welcome to come in and take a look around. I wouldn't think you're a security threat. And if you've lost yer da . . .'

Hal gulped at that.

The little glass window slid to again and the security man went back to his paper.

'Let's go in,' I said to Hal.

'Let's not,' said Hal, hanging back.

'Hal, whatever has happened, it's our fault.'

'No, it isn't,' said Hal fiercely. 'He's a grown-up. He gets called out to jobs all the time. He should be able to look after himself. If he can't, it's not our fault.'

Anyone could pick holes in that argument, but what was the point? I didn't even try. I really wanted my breakfast, and the best way to get it was to sort out this mystery.

'Look, Hal, let's just try to find out what's going on, and then we can go and get some food.'

'All right,' he muttered.

We went in the pedestrian gate and we followed the sign round to the physiotherapy department. Then we came to a little wooden sign, shaped like a finger.

Mortuary, it said, in spooky writing.

'This way,' I said and we went in the direction the sign pointed.

Sure enough, there was the long, low building with a green door.

'You've been here before, Hal,' I said, suddenly realizing that he must have been. Otherwise, he wouldn't have been able to give such detailed instructions in the phone message.

Hal nodded, but he said nothing.

There was a concrete ramp up to the green mortuary door, with a metal rail beside it.

I went up the ramp and tried the handle. It moved downwards very easily, but it had no effect.

I pushed and the door stayed unmoved. I pushed again and still it stuck.

'Locked,' I said, relieved. I hadn't really fancied actually going in there.

'Now what?' asked Hal, looking around. There was nothing much to see, only buildings and drain-pipes and a clutter of bins in one corner.

'We'll have to try looking in the windows,' I said.

'No!' said Hal. 'I'm not peeping in windows at a lot of dead bodies.'

He had a point, I suppose. And anyway, the windows were very high up. You'd need a ladder to look in. That reminded me.

'Well then,' I said, 'in that case, we need to find the van.'

We looked all around. There were lots of places where you might easily park a little van, but no sign of the van we were after. We went round every corner, and when we looked round every corner, there was no little white van. It really was very mysterious. We walked up and down alleyways and behind buildings. We checked the visitors' car park and the staff car park and the consultants' car park. No white van. We looked along a yew-lined, gravelly roadway leading away from one of the car parks. A few cars had been parked there, even though the car park was fairly empty. But no little white van.

'There's no point in hanging around here,' Hal said.

‘No,’ I said, ‘I suppose there isn’t. Let’s go and get some food.’

I was reluctant to leave all the same. As long as we were in the hospital grounds, we had some chance of spotting the van, or Alec, but once we set off for town, the world was just too big; there was too much room for uncertainty. And yet, if I didn’t eat something soon, I knew I was going to collapse. My knees were wobbling already with hunger.

We went back out through the pedestrian gateway and unlocked the bikes. The security man looked up as we rattled the chains. He gave us a friendly little wave.

We waved back.

Chapter 9

We met this guard as we cycled back towards town. He was coming towards us on a bicycle. He was one of those cool guards, in shorts and a cycling helmet and a shiny yellow top.

He raised his hand when he saw us. I suppose it was because we were on bikes; he probably thought we were all part of some big Cycling Movement or something like that, all soulmates or kindred spirits.

I don't know what possessed me, it must have been the friendly little salute, but I gave him a desperate wave and shouted, 'Guard!' at him.

He put a foot under him and skidded to a halt a few metres beyond us. I got off my bike and walked it back to him. Hal put his foot down and looked over his shoulder.

'What can I do for you, young lady?' asked the guard.

'Well,' I said, 'we sort of – eh – lost someone.'

Hal gave a strangulated little cry, but I ignored him.

'We saw him driving into the hospital,' I said. 'But he never came out.'

'Well,' said the guard, 'this does happen. It might not be a case of loss. I mean, was he sick, for example? Or going to visit someone? Or is he a doctor or what?'

'He's a painter,' I said.

'Ah,' said the guard with a grin. 'A painter. Was he going to paint the hospital?'

'That's right,' I said. 'At least, that's what he thought he was doing, only they weren't actually expecting him, see.'

'Right,' said the guard. 'Hmm. Is there any more you can tell me?'

'No,' I said. 'That's it. I was just wondering, how long do you have to be missing before you are a Missing Person?'

'Well, it depends,' said the guard. 'How long has this person been missing?'

'About three-quarters of an hour,' I said.

'That long, eh?' said the guard. I could see he thought this was funny.

'It may not sound very long,' I said, 'but it is very mysterious.'

'Indeed,' said the guard. 'I see.' He didn't see at all.

'And who is the Missing Person?' asked the guard.

'His stepfather,' I said, pointing at Hal.

The guard suddenly looked a bit more serious. Seems if you've just mislaid a miscellaneous someone, it's kind of funny, but if it's a parent, that's a different matter.

'And did ye try ringing him? I take it he has a mobile phone?'

'Eh, no,' I said. 'I mean, yes, he has, but we didn't.'

We couldn't very well ring him, I thought. We weren't supposed to know anything about this visit to the hospital. As far as he was concerned, we were still at home having our breakfasts, and anyway, Hal didn't even talk to him, much less ring him up. But I couldn't tell the guard that. It was all too complicated.

'Well,' said the guard. 'That'd be the first move, I'd say. The mobile phone.'

Then he peered at Hal. 'Are you . . . ?' he called.

Hal stared at him. He looked a bit scared.

'Ah no, you're much bigger,' the guard said.

Hal went on staring. He had started to shiver, though it wasn't very cold. A bit breezy, maybe.

'And, sure, it was years ago. But then, of course, you *would* be much bigger, wouldn't you?'

He made about as much sense as Hal does on a bad day.

'It *is* you, isn't it?' the guard went on.

'He's himself all right,' I said, since Hal wasn't

making any attempt to answer these very peculiar questions.

'You're the little lad whose d– . . . Hal, that was his name. Are you Hal?'

Hal nodded.

The guard grinned, pleased with himself to have worked it out. Whatever 'it' was. 'Stepfather, eh?' he said. 'Well, that's great, so it is.'

Hal still said nothing.

'Well, well,' said the guard. 'It's a small world.'

Which is rubbish. It's a very big world. It's Balnamara that is small, not the world.

'So tell me,' said the guard, 'will yiz be all right now, for getting home? I mean, do you need . . .'

'Oh, we're grand,' I said. 'We were just a bit puzzled. He's probably gone ahead home. It's not a problem. We'll find him. You're right, he's probably not missing at all.'

'Ye're not lost yerselves, are ye? Ye know the way home?'

'Oh yes. It's only about a mile and we have our bikes,' I said cheerfully.

'Only, I . . . I could get a ban-gharda for yiz, if ye need any kind of . . .'

Oh lordy, I thought. He thinks we're helpless. And now he's responsible for us, because we've told him we've lost our adult.

'No,' I said firmly. 'We'll be fine, guard, thank you. We know our way home.'

'If you're sure,' he said doubtfully.

What age did he think we were? About seven, I'd say.

'Positive certain,' I said, with as big a grin as I could manage. I can do sweet little girl if I have to.

'Right,' he said and hopped back on to his saddle. 'If you really are sure. Now, listen to me, if this gentleman doesn't turn up by, say, this evening, you can come back to us. Give the station a ring. Or get your mam to do it, OK? It's probably fine, but you never know, do you? You can't be too careful.'

I nodded. 'Yes, we'll do that. We'll definitely let you know if he doesn't show up.'

'Right,' said the guard.

'Right,' said I.

'Safe home, so!' he called as he pedalled off.

'What do you think you are doing?' shrieked Hal as soon as the guard had disappeared. 'Telling the *guards* about it! Are you out of your tiny mind?'

I thought he was overreacting. I'd only asked for a smallish piece of information.

'It wasn't "the guards". It was one guard.'

'It's all the same,' said Hal.

'Hal, he has disappeared, you know. He was there, and then he wasn't there, and . . .'

'But he's not *missing*! He's just . . . we just don't know where he went. Maybe he met a person he knew. Maybe he came across the canteen and thought he'd have some breakfast. Anything might have happened.'

'Exactly,' I said. '*Anything*. And I don't know about you, but in my family, if you are in trouble, you talk to a policeman.'

'We're not in trouble, Olivia. Not what you would call trouble.'

I wasn't so sure about that.

Just then, a squad car came zipping by, going *whee-hoo*, *whee-hoo*, with its blue light flashing and spinning.

Hal went paler than pale. I thought, if he goes any paler, I am going to be able to see through his skin and see all his bones and veins and everything with the blood all pumping around. He really doesn't like the police. Anyone'd think he was a criminal or something.

The squad car came skidding to a halt at the hospital gate and our friend in the glass kiosk didn't wait to hear what the story was. He lifted the red and orange pole and the squad car revved up again and disappeared into the hospital grounds spitting up a shower of gravel as it went.

'Well!' I said. 'What's all that about, would you think?'

'They . . . ohmyGod, Olivia,' Hal said. 'They must be – arresting Him. That'd be – that'd be cool, Olivia; if he had to go to jail, that'd solve everything. I mean, my mother wouldn't want to marry a criminal, would she? And he might be in jail for *years*. I wouldn't have to go to boarding school; it'd just be me and her, like it used to be.'

Of course, it would solve nothing. Hal was getting a bit carried away.

'Why would they do that?' I asked. 'He hasn't committed a crime.'

'I don't know,' he said. 'Impersonation or something.'

'But he isn't impersonating anyone,' I said. 'It was Larry that did the impersonating, and anyway, you can't really impersonate Clem Clanger, because he doesn't exist.'

'Callaghan, Olivia. Clem Callaghan.'

'It doesn't matter what he's called, he still doesn't exist. You can't impersonate a made-up person, can you?'

'Well, for something else then,' Hal said. 'Maybe they're arresting Him for trying to get into the mortuary under false pretences.'

'But that's not a crime, is it?' I asked.

It didn't look great all the same, did it? First this funny little fellow with colouredy letters all over his van and a shiny face arrives at the local hospital and starts looking for the mortuary with no sensible explanation for why. And then a guard arrives on a bicycle and accuses Hal of being himself only bigger, and then a squad car comes *whoo*-ing by and zooms into the hospital. It was all a bit unsettling, I have to say.

'How do you know what is a crime or what isn't?' Hal said. 'It might be.'

'The guard was right, though, Hal. We should try ringing him. Maybe there is a perfectly innocent explanation.'

'But I never ring Him,' Hal said.

'Still, we could just hang up if he answers.'

'What'd be the point of that?'

'Well, at least we'd know he is alive. And not in custody. I mean, if you have been arrested, you probably wouldn't be allowed to answer your mobile, would you? I'd say it's worth a try.'

The phone rang five times. Then it clicked into the voicemail system.

Uh-oh. My words hung in the air. If you have been arrested, you probably wouldn't be allowed to answer your mobile, would you?

'Maybe he just didn't get to it in time,' I said. 'Let's try again.'

This time the voicemail came on immediately. We didn't bother leaving a message.

Chapter 10

We cycled on into town and stopped at The Muff'nery, which is Balnamara's idea of a cute name for a baker's.

'I hope you have money, Hal,' I said as we dismounted and locked our bikes. 'Because I have hardly any, but if I don't get something to eat, I am going to just drop dead here on the spot and you will have to sling my body over your handlebars and carry me home and explain to my parents how you let me starve to death.'

'Don't be ridiculous,' said Hal. He was counting out his coins. 'I have enough for two bagels and two chocolate muffins. I don't think they do doughnuts here. Will that be OK? I'll get an orange juice as well.'

'That sounds like heaven,' I said. Truth to tell, even a piece of sliced pan with no butter would have been perfectly all right.

We took our goodies to the Market Square and sat on a bench for our little picnic. It's not a market square any more, it's like a little park. There's a monument to some dead poet in the middle, with these benches all around it, and flower beds with busy Lizzies in all sorts of zany colours.

Bagels never tasted so good. I didn't even mind about not having any butter or jam.

'Give me your mobile, will you?' I said to Hal. 'I have to ring home. They're bound to be back from the airport by now, and they'll be wondering where I've got to. I'll tell them we're on a project for school. It's a bit lame, but we have to say something. I'll be murdered anyway, but I'd be murdered even worse if I didn't phone in.'

'You should have your own mobile,' Hal said grudgingly, but he handed his over all the same.

'My parents don't approve of children with mobiles,' I told him, for the umpteenth time. 'They explained it to me once, but I've forgotten the reason.'

'But it's OK if you use mine?' Hal said grumpily. 'That doesn't make sense.'

He'd got very edgy, ever since Alec got arrested. Maybe arrested. I suppose he thought his mother was going to be very upset. Well, you would be, wouldn't you? Upset, I mean, if your son had organized to have your sort-of-husband arrested on a Saturday morning. Even if it wasn't exactly planned that way.

'It's the principle,' I said, 'not the radiation. It's

like not being allowed to watch much TV. Don't worry, I'll buy you some credit later.'

I never did buy him that credit because I forgot, but now that I have remembered it, I think I won't buy it anyway. He got us into this situation; the least he could do was cover the cost of a phone call to let my parents know we hadn't been kidnapped.

'Do you want to ring *your* mother?' I asked him, after I'd had a very strained conversation with mine.

'No,' he said in a surly voice.

'Hal, you have to tell her you're OK.'

'I don't,' Hal said. 'Anyway, she's not even there.'

'She has a mobile,' I argued.

'But she doesn't know I'm not at home. And anyway, she doesn't ring me up every time she is out. So I don't see why I have to phone her.'

'Well,' I said, 'I see why. She could be ringing your house all morning and wondering why there is no one home. I'm going to ring her if you won't. I'll tell her you're with me.'

'If she wants to talk to me,' said Hal, 'which she doesn't, she will ring me on my mobile.'

'All the same, you have to cover yourself,' I said, dialling Hal's home number. 'You can't just walk out of the house and not leave any word about where you are.'

'Oh, hi, Mrs De– . . . I mean, Mrs Ki– . . . well, whatever, eh, Trudy,' I trilled. (I really did trill. I was doing my best to sound cheerful.) 'It's me, Olivia. Just wanted to let you know that Hal's with me; we're on this sort of project thing, you know, Explore Your Area or something it's called, for . . . for SESE, that's what was called history'n'geography, I think, when you were at school. And science. We have these, like, worksheets and we have to find all these monuments and stuff, raths and statues and everything, so . . . anyway, I think he forgot to tell you he'd be . . . oh, he's at the toilet at the moment, which is why I'm ringing, OK? We're just by the poet statue now, actually, in the square. We've ticked that one off our list. Oh, there's the pip, well, byeee!'

'What'd she say?' Hal asked when I rang off.

'Oh, she didn't answer. I was just leaving a message.'

'It's a nice day,' Hal said after a moment. 'We could go to the strand and fly the kite. After we've finished the muffins.'

'Hal, we could NOT! We have to rescue your stepfather.'

'He is not my stepfather,' said Hal. 'And we can't rescue him. We're just a couple of kids. And anyway, he most probably doesn't need rescuing.'

'He does if he's been arrested,' I said. 'Oh, Hal, just think, if Alec has been arrested because of *us* . . .'

'It's not because of us,' said Hal. '*We* didn't get

him arrested.' His voice had got higher than usual, and squeaky. He was definitely ruffled, I thought. 'He got *himself* arrested, the silly galoot. If he has been. Which he probably hasn't been.'

'Still, all those police . . . That's very odd, Hal, wouldn't you say? We really had better find out what the situation is, don't you think?'

'How?' asked Hal.

'We'll have to go to the Garda station and find out.'

'What!'

'You heard me, Hal. We have to go and see if we can find out if he's been arrested.'

'But – we can't just go swanning into the Garda station and ask if they have Him,' said Hal. 'Because if they have, they will want to know what we know about it, and then . . . And anyway, I don't want to see that guard again, the one that thinks he knows me.'

'We have no choice, Hal.'

'We have a choice,' said Hal. 'We can just forget about Him and go and fly the kite.'

That was all just talk, I knew. I could see that he was starting to get worried. There were two little pink spots high up on his cheeks, as if someone had kissed him, twice. Not even Hal could have wanted his little plan to have been quite this effective. All he'd meant to do was create a row between his mother and Alec. He hadn't actually planned on getting anyone arrested. He was just bluffing when he suggested flying the kite.

'Hal! If you were an idiot, which would you be, a bit of a fool or a complete moron?'

He got the message, I think. Though it's hard to tell with Hal sometimes. He slumped back on the bench and took a vicious bite out of his muffin.

'I suppose we could be on a school project,' I went on, 'and just meet him by chance, while we're looking around the station.'

'I don't think you could wander into a cell by chance,' said Hal. 'I believe they lock the doors.'

'Funny that,' I said and gave a nervous little giggle.

Hal smiled. It was the first smile he'd given all morning. It made me feel better. Not much better, but a bit better.

'Come on, Hal,' I said then, wringing the bakery bags into a knot for putting in the litter bin. 'Let's go. We have to see a policeman about a dog.'

'What dog?'

'Oh, Hal. No dog. It's only a turn of phrase. We just have to go and see a policeman.'

'It might be a woman,' Hal argued.

Well, that was true, but really, sometimes I could shake Hal. He comes up with the most pointless remarks. True, but pointless.

'It might,' I said, with a sigh.

And as a matter of fact, it was.

Chapter 11

When we got to the station, I went in. Hal stayed outside, 'to keep an eye out,' he said.

It wasn't very nice in the Garda station; everything was grey and the walls were very bare and there were crumpled papers on the floor, which was covered in worn tiles. The place seemed to be empty, but there was a little bell on the counter, so I gave it a ring. It made a mighty buzzing sound, enough to wake the dead, you'd think, but it didn't seem to have any effect.

I waited for ages, and I was just wondering if I should ring again, or would that annoy them, when this young guard came out and asked what she could do me for (ho-ho).

She had a nice smile, so I didn't bother making anything up or saying I was on a project or anything, I just asked her straight out about Hal's stepfather. She gave me a funny look, as if she thought I didn't seem to be the kind of person who knows people who get arrested (which is true), but she went off and came back with a sheaf of papers.

'I have no record of anyone of that name,' she said, wrinkling her nose in puzzlement.

That was a relief.

'You mean, he hasn't been brought here?' I said.

'No, I mean he hasn't been arrested this morning at all. He's not on our list. That kind of information is instantly available, you know.'

'Really?' I said faintly.

'Oh yes. We have the latest technology.'

'Oh!' I said. 'Well, thank you, guard.'

That was good news. It didn't explain what had happened, but at least we hadn't got a person arrested for nothing. I bounced out to where Hal was sitting on a wall outside the station.

'He's not here,' I said.

'Does that mean he hasn't got here yet?'

'No, it means he hasn't been arrested.'

'Oh well,' said Hal. He stood down from the wall and dusted his hands smartly together. 'Well, now we know.'

'Thanks for asking, Olivia,' I said. 'You are a fine friend and I owe you a big favour.'

'Who are you talking to?' Hal said.

'Myself,' I said.

'You're nuts,' said Hal.

I sighed. 'I must be,' I said. 'OK then, what

now? And do NOT mention that kite, Hal King, or I will . . . Oh! *Hal!*' I shrieked.

It was using Hal's full name that made me realize what an idiot I'd been.

'What?' he asked. 'What, what? What's wrong?'

'No, nothing's wrong,' I said, 'or maybe it is. Oh no!'

'Olivia, could you please talk sense?' Hal pleaded.

'I've just realized,' I said. 'I used the wrong name in the Garda station. I asked for Alec *King*, not Alec Denham. I keep forgetting he doesn't have the same name as you – remember, I couldn't think what to call your mother on the phone; gee, that was dead embarrassing, did you notice?'

'So . . .'

'So,' I said, 'we are none the wiser. He might have been arrested after all. Oh, Hal. Sorry.'

I felt such a dumb-cluck, and I really didn't fancy the idea of going back in there and explaining myself, no matter how nice the policewoman had been.

'Will you come in with me this time?' I asked Hal. 'Please?'

He nodded.

So the two of us stumbled into the reception area and rang the bell again, and after the usual delay, out came my friend.

'I . . . eh, I made a mistake the last time,' I said, grinning dementedly at her in the hope of making her think I was a sweet child that she should be nice to.

'Oh?' she said and she took a pencil from behind her head. She had her hair held up with it, I think, because it all came tumbling round her shoulders when she took the pencil out. She tapped her front tooth with the blunt end. 'What kind of a mistake?'

She had a nice face. With her hair down, she looked quite young. Well, I mean, she still looked like an adult, but as if she hadn't been one all that long. She probably didn't think I was a sweet child, but she looked as if she might be sound.

'A name mistake,' I said.

'Let me get this straight,' she said and she tapped her tooth again. Then she turned the business end of the pencil towards me, as if I was a chart she wanted to point something out on. 'You came in here to ask about an arrest and you didn't even *know the name* of the arrested person? Alleged arrested person.'

She poked the pencil towards me in an unnecessarily menacing way.

'That's . . . well, I did know. I just . . .'

'You know we can't be handing out information about arrests to just anyone. It'd have to be a person with a genuine reason.'

The pencil poked the air in front of my nose again.

'Oh, I have a genuine reason,' I said.

'I mean, a reason *we* would consider genuine,' she said sternly.

'Yes,' I said. 'I understand.' I licked my lips nervously. They tasted of chocolate muffin. I hoped my tongue wasn't all brown. I tucked it quickly back into my mouth.

'So who is this person you are looking for information about?' she asked officiously, licking the point of the pencil and holding it over a sheet of paper. 'Is it a member of your family?'

'No,' I said. 'It's a member of *his* family.' I pointed at Hal. I was glad I'd got him to come in this time. 'But he's too shy to ask himself.'

'Ah, I see,' she said. 'Well, that's understandable. Now, what's this gentleman's name? If you have quite decided, that is.'

'Denham,' I said.

'Denham,' she said and wrote it down.

Well, at least she hadn't suddenly shrieked in recognition. That looked good.

'First name?'

How many Denhams did she think might have been arrested in Balnamara in the last hour and a half? But I didn't say that. I just said, 'Alexander.'

'And are you a Denham too?' she said, turning to Hal.

'Nuh-o,' he stammered. 'I'm a King.'

'You don't look like a king,' she said and laughed.

Hal has heard this joke before. He didn't smile.

'Not even a prince,' she went on.

Still there was no reaction from Hal.

'What's your first name?' she asked, more gently.

'Hal.'

'And you're sure you're not a King?'

'I am; it's a Denham I'm not.'

'Oh, right, yes, I see. And what is Hal short for? Hallelujah?'

I started to giggle.

'Haldane,' muttered Hal.

I giggled some more at that. She frowned at me, but it looked like a frown she'd just put on, like a mask.

'I can't help it,' said Hal. 'It was my mother's idea.'

The guard gave a little tinkly laugh. But then she frowned again and said crisply, 'People in the same family usually have the same surname. Is this man some in-law of yours or what? Or a cousin maybe, on the mother's side?'

'Nuh-o,' stuttered Hal.

'Good. For a moment there I was under the impression you were related to this person. The one you say was arrested.'

We hadn't said that. We'd only asked if he had been. But I thought we shouldn't argue. She wasn't such a walkover as I had hoped she was going to be. Being children, and moderately cute, wasn't working the way it does with some adults.

'Well?' I said, after a moment. 'What is . . . I mean, can you tell us . . . ? I mean, what's the . . . situation?'

She opened up the top of the counter and jerked her head. 'You'd better come into the day room and have a cup of tea,' she said. 'I'm just going off duty, so we can have a chat without being disturbed. One of the others will be minding the shop.'

Maybe she was going to be OK.

I looked at Hal. He was very pale and the two little pink spots on his cheeks looked even pinker.

He shrugged at me. I shrugged at him. Then we both trooped in behind the counter and went into this room they have behind the scenes. I wondered why it was called the day room. Then I wondered if they had a night room too. Maybe not. Maybe it's like the Low Strand, even though there isn't any High Strand.

There were a few other guards sitting around. Two of them were playing cards and one in a corner was doing something on a computer. I recognized the guard on the computer as the bicycle guard we'd met earlier. He gave me a big grin and a wave.

Uh-oh, I thought. Now he's going to know why we're here, and could we not find our way home, and is this man still missing, and . . . but he didn't say anything. He went back to what he had been doing.

Our guard pointed to a sofa that had seen better days. It looked as if the dog slept on it, actually, but beggars can't be choosers. (That's another of my mother's annoying little sayings; it's funny how these things rub off on you, even if they annoy you.) So we sat down, side by side, on the manky sofa. There was a horrible little brown table in front of it. I stared at an application form for a passport that was lying on it, and our guard went out of the room for a moment and came back with two cans of Coke and two teacups.

'The kettle is stone cold,' she said. 'I thought you might prefer this anyway.'

She thought right. She was pretty deadly really.

'Now,' she went on as we poured our Coke into the cups, 'I want to hear the whole story from the beginning.'

'Will you tell, Hal?' I asked. 'Seeing as it's your story.'

But I could see he really didn't feel like telling the story. His face was white and I thought I could hear his teeth chattering, though that might have been just the Coke, which was very cold.

'All right,' I said, when Hal shook his head. 'I'll explain.'

So I did. The guard began by writing down everything I said, but the further I got into the story, the more slowly she wrote, and eventually she put down her pencil and notepad and just listened. She shook her head a few times, and once or twice she groped in a tissue box for a paper hanky and did the most tremendous amount of coughing and spluttering into it.

'So we got my brother to leave the message on the answering machine,' I said, 'and he must have got it, Mr Denham, I mean, because he set off this morning and he drove to the hospital and he went in. We followed him, just for the laugh, like, well, actually, we didn't follow, we went ahead and waited for him, but anyway, we saw him going in the hospital gate. And the next thing was a squad car arrived. And he didn't come out, and we couldn't work out what was going on.'

She shook her head about fifteen times, and then she said, 'So, because of you two and yer – *prank*,' said our guard, 'the guards have arrested, as far as you know, an innocent man who only wanted to paint a building in the hospital? This boy's step-father, is it?'

Hal opened his mouth, but I didn't want him explaining how Alec wasn't really his stepfather, so I said quickly, 'Yes, that's about it, I suppose.'

'Well,' the guard said briskly, 'you are the boldest children I ever met. Ye deserve to go to jail, the pair of ye.'

I could see that the edges of her mouth kept wanting to turn up in a smile, but still, I wasn't sure if we could trust her not to make life difficult for us.

'It was his idea,' I said.

That was mean of me, I suppose, and I am not proud of it, but it *was* his idea. I hadn't liked it in the first place, as you may remember, and it didn't seem fair if I had to go to jail for something I hadn't wanted to get involved in from the start. (Though I suppose a lot of criminals say that.)

'But luckily for you,' she said, ignoring me, 'you are too young for jail.'

Well, we kind of knew that, but all the same, when you are more or less in police custody, it's nice to hear it from the horse's mouth, so to speak.

'Thank you, guard,' I said humbly.

'But tell me one thing,' she said. 'Tell me why.'

'Why what?'

'Why did you do it? Why did you want to play such a trick on this poor man?'

'Well . . .' I said and I looked at Hal.

I certainly wasn't going to tell her it was part of a major plot on Hal's part to make his mother split up with his stepfather, and that I had gone along with it out of a misguided commitment to saving the earth from global warming.

'I mean, it isn't even April Fool's Day,' the guard was saying. 'If it had been the first of April, of course we'd have been expecting this sort of thing.

The hospital sometimes gets dragged into tasteless pranks like that.'

I had a wild idea that I would say it was a kind of dress rehearsal for April Fool's Day, but it was June, for heaven's sake. It wouldn't have been very convincing. So I said nothing, just took another sip of my Coke. It tastes different out of a teacup, for some reason.

'Well . . .' said Hal and he cleared his throat.

We both looked at him. He seemed to have shrunk since earlier that morning. His jumper looked too big for him.

'My dad . . .' he said. 'Not Him, my own dad . . .'

Uh-oh, weirdsville, I thought. What has your *dad* got to do with anything? But I didn't say it out loud. I remembered how he'd gone a bit moochy when the security man at the hospital had mentioned him losing his da, and then how pale he'd got when we'd been talking to the bicycle guard. I hoped he wasn't going to do anything embarrassing.

I fixed my eyes on the passport application form on the table. It was upside down, but I could read it if I concentrated.

'Yes?' said the guard. She had gone very still, very listening.

There was a long silence.

I deciphered the whole passport form while I

was waiting for Hal to say something else. You'd be amazed the personal information they want just to give you a passport. People have no privacy, have they?

Two of the guards, the ones who had been playing cards, stood up and put on their caps and said goodbye to everyone and went out. Still Hal hadn't said any more.

The door closed behind the two guards and the silence settled in again.

At last Hal spoke. 'He died on a Friday,' he said.

His voice was really tiny, as if it belonged to a minute little creature. A beetle, maybe, or a caterpillar, something not only small but also usually not at eye level with you and rather far away.

'I'm sorry to hear that, Hal,' the guard said quietly.

Behind me, I could hear the squeak and creak of the swivel chair the guard at the computer was sitting on. He'd stopped tapping at the keyboard. It was as if the whole room was holding its breath.

Our guard sat with her hands together on her knees, the fingers intertwined, and she waited to see if Hal was going to say any more.

'When I was small,' Hal said, 'we flew a kite once, the two of us. That's the only thing I remember about him. That and about it being a Friday when he died.'

Friday. Something clunked in my brain. It wasn't like a piece of a jigsaw clicking into place, the way people say. It was more like someone dropping a very heavy suitcase on a wooden floor in the room above you, thunk, and it's so heavy, it kills its own vibrations.

'I see,' said the guard. 'That's very sad for you, Hal.'

'Yes,' said Hal.

There was another silence and then Hal added, 'I found him.'

'Oh, Hal,' I breathed.

I had never heard this before. This was the Something Awful that had happened. It was awfuller than I'd thought.

The guard gave me a look. Don't say a word, her look said.

'I don't remember that part,' Hal was saying. 'I was only five. My mother told me; that's how I know.'

The swivel chair squeaked again. I wished I was somewhere else, somewhere noisy and cheerful, like a café or a schoolyard at playtime.

'Except,' Hal said, and he sounded as if this had only just occurred to him for the first time, 'except his shoes. I remember his shoes. Very shiny. Like polished chestnuts.' His voice got quieter. 'I'd forgotten that.' The last sentence was as if he was talking to himself.

I shuffled on my chair. Shoes, kites, death. I didn't really want to be listening to this stuff.

The guard waited for a bit longer, but Hal didn't say any more. I could hear a clock ticking. I looked over my shoulder and saw a big one on the wall overhead. Every time the second hand moved, the clock gave a tick.

After a while, the guard said, 'I went to China on my holidays last year.'

Oh no! I thought. Another weirdo. What is it about me that I keep meeting weirdos? I must have a kind face. That's probably it. I must look like the sort of person it's OK for weirdos to dump on with their weirdnesses.

Anyway, I must have coughed or giggled or something, because the guard looked at me, but she didn't seem to see me. It was as if she was thinking about something else, something that wasn't there.

She fished in her pocket and took out a scrunchy and started to make a ponytail of her hair. It was thick and shiny; it made a lovely ponytail. I wish I had straight hair.

'My dad came too, can you believe it?' the guard said, swinging her ponytail. 'I hadn't been on holidays with my dad since I was your age, and that's a long time ago. But he was so lonely after my mam died, I thought it'd be nice for him to get away, and you can't get much further away than China, can you?'

'Right,' I said. Loony, I thought.

'I have great photos. Only they're at home. Of us flying kites, I mean. Sorry, I should have explained that first. That's what reminded me, Hal, when you mentioned . . .'

'Oh?' I said. 'Oh, I see.' Well, it did make a tiny bit of sense, I suppose, once she explained she'd been flying kites with her dad.

'It's a thing called the Festival of Pure Brightness,' she said. 'He loved the kites.'

'Nice,' I said, in a false, bright voice. I couldn't think of anything else to say. Sometimes 'nice' is the best you can do. This was the weirdest conversation I'd had in a very long time.

'Yeah, nice,' said Hal. And they gave each other shy little goofy smiles. 'The Festival of Pure Brightness. Sounds – eh, bright.'

Yeah, right, Hal, I thought. Sounds bright. Sounds pure. Sounds Chinese. Sounds as if we should be getting along home now.

She didn't ask any more questions about the business at the hospital, which was dead-on of her, because Hal really hadn't explained.

'I dunno, I dunno,' she said after a while, standing up and bustling about a bit. 'What are we going to do with ye at all?' She crushed the two Coke cans and gathered up the sticky cups.

'What about Mr Denham?' I asked. 'Can you

get them to let him go, now you have the whole story, like?'

'Oh no,' said the guard, standing at the door, with her hands full of the cups and cans.

Blinkin' marvellous, I thought. Now what? I took a quick peek at Hal and he looked close to tears.

'Because he wasn't arrested at all,' the guard went on. 'I checked the first time you were in, and nobody was arrested at the hospital this morning.'

'But there was a squad car!' I said.

'There was. We'd got a message from the hospital that they needed something urgently for a patient. It was coming on the train from Dublin. Some sort of plasma, I think. We sent the squad car to the railway station to get it, and then we zoomed it up to the hospital as fast as we could.'

'Plasma!' I yelped. 'It was just . . . oh!'

Hal gave a huge grin. 'So he hasn't been arrested?'

'No, I told you, no one was arrested. Why on earth did you think he might have been arrested?'

'I dunno,' Hal and I said in unison.

We looked a bit foolish. At least Hal did, and I am sure I looked no different. Foolish, but hugely relieved. Now that we knew Alec Denham hadn't been arrested, it seemed ridiculous that we'd ever thought he might be.

The guard shook her head. 'Ye watch too much telly,' she said.

Maybe she's right. We'd put two and two together and got about a hundred and five. Whew!

'But what happened to him?' I asked, when we'd stopped huffing and blowing with relief. 'I mean, is he still lost in that hospital or what?'

'I wouldn't think so. He probably drove on home.'

'But we never saw him coming out,' I said. 'We waited for ages, didn't we, Hal?'

'I suppose he must have driven on through then,' the guard said.

'How do you mean, "on through"?'

'On through and out the back gate,' she explained.

The back gate! Hal and I stared at each other. His mouth hung open. So did mine. Why hadn't we thought of that? It was so simple.

'That road . . .' I said, but then I clamped my mouth shut, to stop my chin hanging like the bucket of a road-digger.

Hal nodded. '. . . with the trees,' he mumbled.

'We never wondered where it *went*,' I said with a groan. 'We just looked to see if the van was parked on it.'

'We are thick,' said Hal.

'As a brick,' I said.

'As two bricks,' said Hal.

'As a whole houseful of bricks,' I said.

'Ah, not really,' said the guard. 'It's hardly ever

used, because it comes out on to a very bad boreen, all potholes. People don't even know it's there half the time, but if you follow that little gravelly road, you end up at the back gate.'

I don't know why the security man didn't say anything about the back gate, but he hadn't been all that helpful anyway. Maybe it just didn't occur to him any more than it did to us.

'So you mean,' I said to the guard, 'while we've been sitting here telling you the whole story, he's at home watching the races?'

'I suppose so,' said the guard cheerily. 'If that's how he normally spends his Saturdays.'

How could we have been so *stupid*!

'And we've been through all this for nothing?'

'Well, I wouldn't say that,' said the guard. 'I'd say you had some explaining to do.'

'Sorry, guard,' I said and I gave Hal a little kick on the ankle. Not really a kick, more a nudge with the side of my foot.

'Yeah, sorry, guard,' he said.

She smiled and then she pushed the door open with her hip and disappeared for a moment.

When she came back, she said, 'Now, will I send you home in a squad car or what?'

'No!' I squawked.

Bad enough to be thick, stupid, idiotic nincompoops of fools, but we didn't have to look like criminals on top of all that. Can you imagine if we arrived home in a squad car! My mother would murder me. She was going to murder me anyway, but if I came home under Garda escort, she'd really *mean* it.

'Yes!' said Hal at the same time.

Boys are like that. They'd jump at the chance of being zoomed around in a squad car, no matter how it embarrassed their families.

The guard laughed. 'Which is it to be?'

'Please, Olivia,' said Hal. 'Oh, come *on*! A squad car!'

'But we have bikes,' I said. I was never so glad that I had a bike.

'Did you leave them outside?' asked the guard, looking out of the window. 'Only there's no sign of them out there. Surely to goodness they wouldn't steal two bikes from outside the Garda station!'

'No,' I said. 'We left them at the square. Beside the poet statue.'

'That'd be Kavanagh,' she said.

'Oh, is that who it is?'

'Yes,' she said. 'He's my favourite. We did his poems at school. He's famous.'

'I suppose you have to be famous to get a statue,' I said.

'And dead,' said Hal.

'I suppose so,' said the guard. 'It's a way of honouring a dead person, isn't it. I mean, you can't give them a present, can you?'

'Hmm,' said Hal.

I couldn't believe we were having this discussion about dead people and statues when we were going to be driven home in a squad car and be grounded for *life* probably.

'Anyway, look, what about this for a compromise? I'll give you a lift in the squad car as far as the square to pick up your bikes. It's only a few hundred metres, but children who spend their Saturdays wasting Garda time deserve no better. That's an offence, you know.'

I knew she wasn't really threatening us. Just sort of reminding us, I suppose, that you can't go around creating havoc for the guards, even if Something Awful did happen to you.

I found out about Kavanagh afterwards, by the way, because I like poems, even if I'm not that interested in statues. He has a great one about canals and far-flung towns. This'd be a far-flung town, I suppose. Maybe that's why we have a statue of him.

You wouldn't believe how ordinary a squad car is on the inside. The back seat had one of those stretchy covers with a fluffy brown surface on it that people put in their cars; I don't know why – it's pretty horrible. It also had one of those dangling Christmas tree things that smell like the stuff people squirt in the toilet to make it smell like not-toilet.

Our guard sat in the driver's seat and the bike guard, the one who'd been on the computer, got into the front passenger seat. Hal didn't like that, but he couldn't argue. It was their car.

'Will you put on the siren?' he asked, after we'd put our seat belts on.

Our guard laughed, but she was a good sport and she did it.

'Oh *yes*!' said Hal and we sped off in the direction of the Market Square, *whee-hoo*, *whee-hoo*, *whee-hoo*. It was kind of cool, I have to admit.

'Goodbye, so,' said our guard, when we'd climbed out of the squad car. 'And next time,' she added with a grin, 'try to get the name of the person you are enquiring about right. It is much less suspicious.'

'I don't think there'll be a next time,' I said.

I mean, let's face it. How often does someone you know get arrested at the hospital? Nearly arrested even?

She shook both our hands through the window of the squad car and said, 'My name is Sonya O'Rourke. If ye're ever in trouble again, just ask for me, OK?'

'Thanks, Sonya,' said Hal.

I gave him a dig in the ribs. 'Thanks, Guard O'Rourke,' I said.

'Here,' she said, and she took out a notebook and wrote something down in it with her pencil.

Then she tore the page out, folded it over twice and shoved it out the car window at Hal.

'Um, thanks,' said Hal again, looking at the folded note.

We waved them goodbye and she put on the siren again, just for the fun of it.

'Is that her phone number?' I asked Hal, nodding towards the piece of paper. 'She must like you.'

Hal blushed. He scrunched up the piece of paper and stuck it in his pocket.

I really was not looking forward to facing my parents after being out practically all day without permission. They don't like that kind of thing in my family. They get very cranky, in fact.

Chapter 12

Larry phoned from Paris in the morning. After the murder and mayhem there'd been in our house the previous day when I'd got home, I'd nearly forgotten about my Romanesque brother.

'Hey, Larry!' I warbled. 'How's it going? How's Paris? Is it fabulous? Do you get croissants for breakfast? Are you having a great time with the lads? I bet you're having wild parties in your hostel, are you? I wish I was in secondary . . .'

'Great, Liv, it's cool. Look, can I speak to Mum or Dad, please? Urgently?'

'They've gone to church,' I said. 'It's Sunday here. I'm cooking their breakfast, as a peace offering.'

'It's Sunday here too; we've been to Notre Dame,' he said. 'Gothic,' he added, before I told him. 'How come you're at home by yourself? Have they finally caved in to your demands to be recognized as a Free Thinker?'

Wow! My brother the comedian! It must've been

the Parisian air. But, of course, I didn't give him the satisfaction of laughing at his little witticism.

'I'm not,' I said. 'It's just that I'm grounded. Strict house arrest.'

'House arrest! That doesn't include . . .'

'I know, I know,' I sighed. 'Let's not go there, Larry.'

My parents had been furious when I said that I couldn't go to church because that would break the terms of my house arrest, but they hadn't had time to have it out with me, so they'd gone off muttering, 'You haven't heard the last of this, young lady.' 'Young lady' is always a bad omen, I find.

'Why?' asked Larry. 'Why are you under house arrest, as you call it?'

'Because of yesterday and getting Alec – you know, Mr Denham, Hal's sort-of-stepdad – well, we almost got him arrested, me and Hal. And you.'

'Arrested! Olivia, what *happened*?'

'Oh, it's not so bad. We only *thought* he'd been arrested, but really . . .'

Larry interrupted. 'Look, I've just realized this phone call is costing a bomb. You can tell me all this when I get home. So just listen, will you? I've got myself into . . . well, I wouldn't say trouble exactly, but . . .'

Larry in trouble. That was a new concept. I was intrigued.

'Larry, what have you done?'

'Well, um, I'm what you might call up doo-doo creek and there is a serious shortage of paddling equipment.'

Larry is a bit like my mother that way. Tries too hard to be funny and ends up sounding pompous and ridiculous.

'Larry,' I said in exasperation, 'I thought you were in a hurry. Will you just say whatever it is and put me out of my misery?'

'My passport has been stolen.'

'Oh, Larry! You idiot.' I have to admit that I chortled. 'You lost it, didn't you?'

'It doesn't matter, the thing is, it's gone. The teacher said to ring home. We reported it to the French police, but they weren't very interested.'

I shuddered slightly at the mention of the police. I was beginning to feel we were having far too much contact with the law in this family lately.

'So what's going to happen? Are you going to be stuck over there? Poor you, forced to live on *petits pains au chocolat*!'

'I dunno,' said Larry. 'Ask them to phone me when they get home, will you? It's a bit nerve-wracking. Someone told me it's a crime to go out in this country without your papers.'

'What papers?'

'ID,' said Larry. 'Passport.'

'Oh, Larry! Are you going to have to stay stuck inside all the time? Under *hotel* arrest?'

'Well, no,' said Larry. 'I'm going to risk it. Live dangerously, that's my motto.'

That is *so* not Larry's motto! Paris must've been going to his head.

When my parents came back, all set to pick up the row where we'd left off, I told them that Larry was living dangerously in Paris. They didn't see the funny side of it. They got worked up into a right schemozzle about it, and they started ringing around all sorts of people, but because it was Sunday there wasn't very much they could do, except tell Larry to report it to the embassy in Paris first thing the next day.

Luckily, all the flap and hoo-ha about Larry and his missing passport took the heat off me. Of course, they did still make me go to church later in the morning. Parents always win, don't they? Not that I minded. We have a gospel choir. It's cool.

In the end, it turned out there was somebody in the embassy in Paris after all, even though it was Sunday – 'skeleton staff', they called it, spooksville! – and they said not to worry at all, they would be able to do something about Larry's passport, and it turned out he got invited to *dinner* by the ambassador because he was a friend of someone who knew my dad. That is just so Larry. He gets into what should be serious trouble and he ends up getting invited out to a swanky dinner. Things like that never happen to me. I get to drink Coke out of a teacup in a grimy Garda station. Hal too. Then I remembered suddenly all that stuff yesterday about Hal's dad dying and everything. It made drinking Coke out of a teacup seem not so bad really.

Now I come to think of it, it mightn't have been the actual ambassador, but it was definitely one of the high-ups in the embassy.

'Now, if you are offered a glass of wine with your dinner, Larry,' my mother said earnestly into the phone, 'you may take *a small one* and add *a lot* of water to it, but otherwise, no, OK?'

'How come Larry can drink all of a sudden?' I asked.

'He's in France. People have wine with their meals. That doesn't count as "drinking".'

'He was in France yesterday too and it was absolutely no way.'

'Then he was with a group of Irish schoolkids. Now he's going to dinner with the Third Secretary.' (How many secretaries do these ambassador people need? I wondered.) 'It's different.'

'No, it's not,' I said. 'He's still fifteen.'

I don't know, parents have the weirdest attitudes to their own rules. It's like house arrest not applying to going to church. When I grow up, I will be more consistent.

Chapter 13

Hal turned up in the afternoon, with his kite under his arm. My father opened the door. I was watching from the top of the stairs. I could see he was not pleased just by the way he stood there.

'Hello, Mr O'Donoghue,' said Hal. 'Can Olivia come out?'

'No!' barked my dad, but he jerked his head to indicate that Hal could come in to see me. Even prisons allow visitors, don't they?

'What's going on?' Hal whispered as soon as we got into the dining room, which is the best place, because the adults never go in there unless we have people round for dinner, which, of course, doesn't happen on Sunday afternoons.

'Larry's got to go to dinner in a Paris apartment with Irish embassy people,' I said, 'and it's full of over-stuffed cushions, gold silk' – actually, I just made that bit up, but I bet it's very luxurious – 'and it has shutters but they don't open them so it's dark and mysterious and it smells of cat and potpourri. Doesn't that sound adventurous?'

I wished I could go to Paris. I imagined myself about three years older in very pointy high heels and a little black dress in high rooms lined with bookshelves, talking about something serious, philosophy maybe or films, I don't know what, but serious stuff anyway. And people listening to me. That'd be the best part, instead of everyone telling me to act my age one minute and to do as I'm told the next.

Hal shook his head.

'Well?' I asked. 'What happened when you got home yesterday?'

'Eh, well, we had our lunch,' said Hal. 'Waffles and beans.'

'Sounds disgusting,' I said.

'Well, normally it's broccoli and rice cakes: the stuff women eat. And I put a border round the kite, look. I made it out of wallpaper that I found in a skip on our road.'

'Very nice, Hal,' I said.

'I thought about what you said about a blue kite disappearing into the sky, and I thought a red border would make it more visible.'

'Well,' I said. 'It's nice to know you listen to me some of the time. So it's red like Wednesday then?'

'No!' he said. 'Wednesday is a completely different shade of red!'

'Right,' I said. Weirdo, I thought.

He'd attached these two amazing tails to the kite as well. One was made out of an old Christmas decoration, all glittery streamers, and the other one had these paper bows in different colours – purple and yellow and green and red and pink and turquoise and gold. It was gorgeous, and really long, and every bow was a little bit smaller than the one before it, so the whole tail kind of trailed away, right down to the tiniest little mauve bow, not much bigger than a shirt button. He's quite artistic, Hal, when he puts his mind to it.

'It's wicked, Hal,' I said, 'but what *happened*?'

I was dying to know how Hal's folks had reacted to all that business with the hospital, and whether the row between his mother and Alec had continued after she got back from the golf. It was an *interesting* situation.

'I told you.'

'I mean Alec, what did he *say*? Did he mention the hospital business?'

'To me?'

'Well, yes, to you, to your mother, whatever. Did it come up in conversation over the waffles?'

'He doesn't eat waffles, He . . .'

'Hal!'

'What?'

'Look, let's take this in easy stages. When you got home yesterday, who was there?'

'My mother was still out playing golf.'

'Right. And Alec?'

'He was having a beer in the back garden.'

So he was home before Hal. He hadn't got locked into some sort of nightmare in the hospital, going round and round pathetically looking for Clem Clingham and a pot of paint. He must have known about the back gate all along. He'd got one over on us there, even though he probably didn't even know it.

'So you stuck your head out the back door and said . . . oh no, you don't talk to him, so maybe you waved to him or something?'

'Wave to him? No. I just took my bike round the side of the house. I keep it in the back, and he was sitting there on a deckchair, still wearing his painting overalls.'

'And?'

'So I said, "Were you working this morning then? Only I thought you were going to the golf with my mum."'

'Hal! You *spoke* to him!'

'Well, I thought, it's a bit funny to be wearing his overalls when he's not working, and if I don't mention it, it'll look as if I am avoiding it or something, and that might seem a bit suspicious.'

'Well, yes, but I thought you said you never spoke to him! Not since he moved in.'

'Well,' Hal said, 'I never had anything to say to

him before, not really. Nothing important. But it seemed important to say something yesterday, after . . . everything. So I did.'

'OK, so *he* said?' It was hard work getting this story out of Hal.

'"Rrrmph", something like that.'

I wasn't getting very far with this line of interrogation.

'So, when did your mum get home?'

'She didn't.'

'How d'you mean, she didn't come home? She must have been home by bedtime.'

'No.'

'She stayed out all night?'

'Yeah, looks like it.'

'Hal!'

'It tastes sort of like curry paste,' Hal said, peering at the kite.

'What does? Your mother not being there?'

'No!' he said, as if I should know that a thing like that wouldn't have a taste. How would I know what tastes and what doesn't in Hal's weird world?

'The border round the kite,' he said. 'That shade of red. Green curry paste. Funny that, the way the reds and the greens get mixed up. Never thought of that before.'

The kite, the kite, the wretched kite! He couldn't seem to concentrate on anything else. That and his weird, mixed-up senses of colour and taste.

'Hal!' I said again, pretty thunderously, I have to admit.

Hal's shoulders seemed to collapse in towards his chest, and he had that caved-in look he gets when he's upset. His face was like a snowflake that gets stuck on the outside of the window and you're looking at it from the inside, and you know it's going to slither down any minute and then disappear.

'Sorry,' I said, meaning about shouting at him, but he didn't seem to hear. 'Eh – did she ring or anything?' I asked. 'Was she staying with a friend?'

'No.'

'Well, did Alec explain where she was?'

'No.'

'Does *nobody* ever talk in your family?' I could hear myself getting all psychological, like my mum.

'He isn't in my family.'

'Oh, Hal!'

'Can we go to the strand and fly the kite?' he asked.

'No,' I said, 'I can't. I'm not allowed. I'm grounded.'

'Why?' It sounded like the wind, the way he said it, the wind trapped between tall buildings. He must've really needed to go kite-flying.

'Because of yesterday,' I said, 'being out all day. My parents are furious with me. You're lu–' I stopped myself just in time. This boy's mother had

. . . disappeared, it seemed. He was behaving oddly, but could you blame him? Poor Hal, I found myself thinking. Just like my mum is always saying.

Hal's face looked whiter than ever, if that's possible. He's in danger of turning into an angel, I thought, and flying away altogether.

'When are you ungrounded?' he asked.

'I'm afraid to ask,' I said.

We didn't say anything for a while. I admired the kite. Hal just sat there. It looked as if he was working on draining every last drop of blood out of his head and down into his feet. I suppose if you don't know where your mother's gone, it's probably normal to look like that, but I didn't like it. Hal didn't look himself at all.

'Olivia,' he said at last, in that tiny, insecty voice he had yesterday at the Garda station. 'What if my mother doesn't come home?'

I had been thinking exactly that, but I didn't let on to Hal.

'Of course she'll come home, Hal,' I said. 'Mothers don't just disappear. It's in their job description: they have to stick it out.'

'I shouldn't have done that thing with the mortuary, should I? It's all my fault. It was Him that was supposed to leave, not her. I wish . . .'

'Don't be daft, Hal,' I said. 'There's no connection between you playing a silly trick on Alec and your mother not coming home last night. It's because of whatever is going on between them. Nothing to do with you, you'll see. It's just some silly row they're having.'

I don't know much about how grown-ups think, only what I can work out from *EastEnders*. (I am not supposed to watch *EastEnders*, but hey, I have to live in the real world, whatever my parents think of it.) Still, I'd say that it'd take more than someone not going to a golf tournament to make a couple split up, wouldn't it? And anyway, even if she wanted to leave old Alec, Hal's mum wasn't just going to *abandon* Hal, now, would she? No, there had to be another explanation.

'She was banging doors and screeching and everything yesterday morning before she left for the golf thing. She was *furious* with him. It woke me up, all the shouting.'

I have to say, that sounded a bit serious all right; people don't screech in my family, unless they get a fright in the dark or something, but I said, 'Look, Hal, this is probably what happened. She probably had a few drinks after the golf, maybe she won or something and she got carried away, and then she thought she'd better not drive till this morning because she'd be over the limit, wouldn't she? She's probably seen those ads on the telly where you only have to pick up a drink and the next thing there's mangled bodies all over the road.'

Or maybe she had a few drinks all right, I thought, only she *didn't* decide to stay over but instead got into her car and drove it into the ditch. Oh – my – God! She could be lying there with the crows picking her eyes out. But I didn't say that out loud.

'She probably stayed over at the golf club or with a friend or something,' I said. 'She'll be home by teatime. You'll see.'

I kind of hoped that might be true.

'But why didn't she ring?'

'She probably did. I'm sure she would have phoned Alec.'

'He never said.'

'He just didn't mention it to you. Since you're not exactly on chatting terms. It's all very well you two not talking to each other,' I went on, 'but how are you going to know what's going on if you don't *ask*?'

'Yeah,' said Hal. He definitely cheered up a bit at that thought. 'You're right. She must've rung Him, mustn't she? He thought I knew, I suppose, so he didn't mention it. Yeah, that must be it. I *will* ask Him.'

'Good on you,' I said. 'That's the spirit.'

'I'd better get on home then,' he said, 'and see what the story is.'

'OK,' I said.

'See you tomorrow, Olivia.'

'Yeah, tomorrow,' I said. 'No, tomorrow's the bank holiday. See you on Tuesday, you mean. At school.'

'Yeah, well, Tuesday,' he said.

'Bye, Hal,' I called as I closed the front door behind him.

It would all have blown over by Tuesday, I thought comfortably. It was easier to think comfortable thoughts when Hal wasn't sitting there, slumped in a chair and looking lugubrious. His mother would ring by tomorrow for sure, or she'd come home with a long story about a puncture and a missed train or something. It'd be all right. Mothers don't just walk out on their kids. I never heard of such a thing.

Chapter 14

I was wrong. Hal didn't come to school on Tuesday. I couldn't imagine what was going on in his family. I didn't even want to think about it.

Gilda and Rosemarie had had a tiff at the weekend and they both spent Tuesday trying to get me on their side. The two of them take a lot of energy. I spent the day trying to be nice to each of them exactly the same amount, so they couldn't use me as some sort of an excuse in this row they were having. Something about a bottle of nail varnish. I don't really see the point of nail varnish. I did try it once, but it made my fingernails feel all tingly. I didn't like it. But they ended up both blaming me anyway, even though their stupid row had nothing to do with me. It's funny how people do that – blame someone else for their own rows. I've got used to those two, though, and I didn't let it bother me.

I'm not allowed to phone Hal's mobile from our house phone, because it's too expensive, so when

I got home after school that day I phoned his house, but I kept getting the answering machine. I didn't leave a message, because I didn't know who might listen to it.

Nothing happened at school on Wednesday, except that neither Gilda nor Rosemarie would talk to me – by trying to be equally nice to them, I'd somehow managed to offend them both – and Hal didn't come in again.

On Wednesday evening, Larry came home, looking very sheepish. His passport had turned up in the bottom of his rucksack, where he'd hidden it – in case it got lost.

'I spy with my little eye something beginning with "p",' I scoffed.

He didn't think it was funny.

What my parents didn't think was very funny was that he'd got a tattoo while he was away. That was a fairly Gothic sort of move for an old dyed-in-the-wool Romanesque like Larry, I thought. Showing a bit of spirit at last. It was quite a nice one, a sort of birdy creature, a peacock maybe, or a phoenix, winding round his wrist, very dramatic, but it was in a stupid place because it crept right down on to his hand; it would be on show all the time; you couldn't hide it even with a really long-sleeved shirt.

My mother threw a conniption. She wailed, 'Where did I go wrong?'

'You didn't go wrong, Mum,' I explained to her. 'It was Larry's own idea. Don't go blaming yourself. You did your best with him; you can't take responsibility for how he has turned out.'

'Turned *out*!' she snarled, as if I had accused him of being the leader of a chainsaw massacre, when all I was doing was being nice to her, trying to get her to feel better about Larry's little failings, even though I was secretly thinking that, according to her own theories, Larry had probably got the tattoo because of something that had happened to him when he was younger that made him want to be nasty, though I must say getting a tattoo is a fairly mild sort of nasty, in my own opinion, but I suppose from Mum's point of view it is a Big Deal.

I tried to think of something helpful to say. 'A body piercing would be worse,' I said eventually. 'Even one in a place you couldn't see.'

My mother squealed when I said that. 'Take her *away*!' she screeched at my dad, as if I was some sort of a mangy cat or a plague rat or something. And there I'd been, congratulating my family on not screeching. It just goes to show, doesn't it?

'But I only *said* –' I said.

'That's quite enough, young lady,' my dad said.

All in all, I was not having a good week. Life is not very fair sometimes, is it? And that's just *my* life, which by and large is not too bad; it's not even

Hal's, which is pretty well mingin' really, when you compare.

'And there's not a hasp in the house,' Larry muttered in my ear, in a silly, squeaky voice, as I turned on my heel to leave the room with my chin up and a defiant expression on my face.

That did it for the chin up and the defiant expression. I exploded into giggles.

My mother totally overreacted: she threw *three* cushions at me, flink, flonk, flunk. She must have thought that I was giggling at *her*.

'Get *out*!' she roared.

It wasn't my fault, it was Larry being smart, and there I was getting the blame – again. My family don't understand me.

One of the cushions hit me on the ear. If it had been a book or a teacup or something, it could have knocked me out. Lucky it was a sofa she was sitting on and not a bookcase or a coffee table, or I'd have to report her to the social workers.

Chapter 15

On Thursday, Hal finally turned up at school.

He wasn't wearing his school sweatshirt. We haven't really got a uniform in our school, but we do have a school sweatshirt we are supposed to wear. It's wine-coloured, pretty icky, but teachers have absolutely no taste in kids' clothes. You'd think they'd teach them stuff like that at college, wouldn't you? Like, 'Look, it's simple, read my lips: kids don't like wine-coloured things. Blue, turquoise, red, yellow, orange, silver, purple, even black would do, at a push – just not wine, OK? Or not navy or grey or brown or that shade of green that is trying to be brown.' But no, and that is why you have a country full of children who hate their school uniform. I am sure it is bad for us to be made to wear stuff we hate all the time. We will probably turn into fashion slaves when we grow up and spend all our money on Gucci shoes, trying to make up to ourselves for our childhood misery.

Hal had on a blue sweatshirt, with the elbows out, and he was even thinner and smaller and paler than usual. His hair looked as if he hadn't combed it for days. He had a cold sore at the side of his mouth.

'Hal, what's wrong?' I asked him as we were walking home. That was the first chance I got to talk to him all day.

'What do you mean?' he mumbled.

'Hal, you're not yourself. How come your mum let you wear that sweatshirt to school? You're lucky Mrs Moriarty didn't see you or you'd have been in trouble.'

Mrs Moriarty is our school principal and she is medium scary, about five or six on a scale of one to ten. Her scariness is not because she is exactly horrible, apart from being utterly obsessed with the school sweatshirt, but mainly because she is very tall – and tall is scary when you are a small person. She makes it worse by wearing high heels, really noisy ones. Kate, now, our teacher, is not scary at all, about minus two, and she doesn't give a fig about the school sweatshirt. I don't know why it is a fig that people don't give about things, never a plainer fruit, like an apple or a banana.

'I couldn't find the right one,' Hal said, meaning about the sweatshirt.

'Have you been sick?' I asked.

He shook his head.

I had to ask the awful question. 'Hal, is your mum still away?'

He nodded.

'So it's just you and Shiny Face at home? Since *Saturday*?'

He said nothing. This was not good, I thought. This was not good at all. I tried to imagine my mother not being there, and I managed to feel quite sad at the thought, even though she had thrown not one but three cushions at me yesterday.

'And . . . when is she coming back?'

'Dunno. Dunno where she is.'

'Does Alec not know either?'

'Doesn't seem to.'

'Hal, you can't just not know where your mother is.' It didn't seem reasonable. It wasn't the way things *were*.

'Well, I don't.'

'Maybe she's lost her memory,' I said.

'Maybe.'

'Or been in an accident,' I said. I didn't want to mention anything worse than that. 'Or both. If you have an accident, you can sometimes lose your memory. It's always happening on *ER*. Sometimes it even happens on the news, so it must be true.'

'Yeah.'

There was silence for a while. We walked on slowly. We came to my estate and I jerked my head towards our house. Hal understood that I was inviting him home to my house for a while. He nodded and we dragged on round the corner and in my front door.

'Hi, Mum!' I yelled as I opened the door. It was one of her days for being home early.

'Hi, Liv!' my mother's voice came from upstairs.

'Will you help me to find her?' Hal asked at last, in his tiny little caterpillary voice, as we took off our school bags in the hall.

'Hal, how could we do that?'

'Will you help me, Olivia?' he said again. 'Please.'

Well, what could I say? There is always 'No', of course, but how can you say to your best friend that you don't really feel like helping him to find the most important person in his life? I do exaggerate sometimes, but you know, a person's mother – that's kind of mega, isn't it? I didn't really have much choice in the matter.

'Here,' I said, handing him my comb. 'Do something about your hair. I can't be seen going about with something that looks like it slept in a hedge.'

'Will you?' he pleaded again as he ran the comb through his hair.

'Well, we'll see,' I said, which is one of those infuriating things my mother says when she doesn't want to answer a question. Sometimes I get these worrying little moments of understanding my mother. Sometimes you just *can't* answer a question.

'Have you tried ringing her?' I asked as we trailed through into the kitchen.

'What kind of an eejit do you think I am?' Hal asked.

'Well, I thought it was a good idea,' I said. I didn't see why he had to be so aggressive.

'That's what I mean. *Of course* I tried phoning her. But I can't get her. She's always forgetting to charge up her phone. I've rung her about twenty times. First she didn't answer, then I started getting her voicemail. Now it just goes boooop.'

The way he said 'boooop', it was a very sad sound, like a wail. I suppose it would be a very sad sound, if your mother wasn't answering her phone for days. I can't imagine it.

'Oh,' I said.

We didn't say anything for a long time after that, just thought and thought. At least, I did, but maybe Hal had given up thinking. He must have been worn out with thinking.

'The thing is,' I said, 'you can't . . . we can't do it by ourselves. Find your mother, I mean, and bring her back. We're only kids.'

'But what else can we do?'

'I think you'll have to get Alec to help you.'

'*Him?*' said Hal.

'Yeah,' I said. 'He's an adult. If you work together, you might think up a plan.'

He shook his head.

'Well then,' I said next, 'in that case, we'll have to ring the police.' That was the result of all my thinking, you see.

Hal didn't look too impressed. 'What for?' he asked.

'Well, your mother is a Missing Person, isn't she? You report those to the police. It's not like when we said we'd lost Mr Denham at the hospital. This is for real.'

Hal looked wretched. 'I can't report my *mother* to the police. What do you take me for?'

'You're not reporting *her*, Hal. You're reporting that she's missing. That's different. I mean, she has been gone for days.'

'But – she's gone off and left me with a person I am not even related to, Olivia. Would you think that's OK? It might be against the law. She might go to jail. I might get taken into care.'

I hadn't thought of it that way.

'I'll get us some orange juice,' I said.

We had the orange juice and then I said, 'Look, Hal, we *have* to report it. I mean, she could be in a hospital or anything.'

'No!' said Hal.

Then I had a flash of inspiration. I get these sometimes. I am very lucky like that.

'Hal!' I said. 'We don't need to ring the actual police. We can ring Sonya.'

'Sonya?'

'Guard O'Rourke, with the ponytail. She'll know what to do.'

'She *is* the actual police, Olivia.'

'Yes, but she's friends with us. It's different. She will tell us what is the best thing to do. She might have some ideas we could follow up ourselves.'

Hal brightened up a bit. He liked Sonya, I knew that.

'And she said to ring her if we were ever in trouble again,' I said. 'I can't think of any bigger trouble than this.'

'OK,' he said. 'But suppose a different guard answers.'

'Oh, we won't ring the station. She gave you her own number, didn't she?'

'Did she?'

'Remember, she wrote it on a piece of paper and you put it in your pocket. Are those the same jeans you were wearing on Saturday?'

They looked as if he had been wearing them since Christmas.

Hal dug into his pockets. Out came his mobile phone, with a piece of chewing gum stuck to the side of it and a lot of fluff from shredded tissues stuck to the gum.

'Yuck!' I said.

He pulled the chewing gum off guiltily and threw it in the bin. He laid the phone on the table and dug a bit more. This time he drew out a leaking biro, also with shredded tissue attached to it, half a packet of chewing gum, unchewed, a few pieces of string, a fistful of coins, some pebbles and finally a scrunched-up piece of lined paper. Everything had sand stuck to it.

I caught the paper by the corner and shook the debris from the inside of Hal's pocket off it. Then I opened it up and smoothed it out on the table in front of me.

The pencil was a bit faded after being bunched up in Hal's pocket for days, and the paper was awfully creased, but I could make it out.

'It's in a foreign language,' I said. 'It says "queuing ming jee".'

I turned the paper over. No phone number, no email address, nothing. Just this stupid foreign thing:

Qing Ming Jie

'Fat lot of good this is,' I said.

'I wonder what language it's in,' Hal said.

'There's a Korean girl in Larry's class,' I said. 'We could ask her. It could be Korean.'

'I don't see why you think that,' Hal said. 'It could be anything. Swahili or Lithuanian or anything.'

'Well,' I said, 'I was trying to look on the bright side. We don't know any Swahilis or Lithuanians, but we do know a Korean. Anyway, it sounds more like Korean than Swahili.'

Hal gave me a funny look. He must have guessed I was bluffing. We did learn the Swahili for 'Happy Christmas' once at school, but I had completely forgotten it, and I couldn't tell you from Adam what Swahili sounds like. It could be almost identical to Korean for all I know, though it probably isn't.

Hal picked up the paper. 'It's not "queuing",' he said. 'It's "king". Maybe it has something to do with my name.'

'No, it isn't "king",' I said, peering over his shoulder. 'It's a "q" not a "k".'

'Maybe that's how they spell it in Swahili. I bet that's it.'

'Or Korean,' I said.

'I'd say it's a clue,' he said. At least for five minutes he wasn't thinking about his mother being missing. 'Or a secret message.'

I took the paper back from him and scrutinized it.

'That's not "king",' I said. 'I knew it wasn't. "Q" sounds like *kw*, not like *k*.'

'Only if there's a "u" after it,' Hal said. 'There's no "u" after this "q".'

'Maybe it's like the airline, Qantas. You pronounce the "u" even though it's not there.'

'Then it'd be "kwing",' Hal said. 'Not "queuing".'

'Let's face it,' I said. 'We haven't a clue. We don't

even know what it means, so I don't see why we are bothering to argue about how to pronounce it.'

'We *have* got a clue,' Hal said. 'This is it, *this* is a clue.'

'To what, though?' I asked. 'It's not going to . . .' I was going to say it wasn't going to help us find Hal's mother, only then I thought that wasn't a great thing to say, because I didn't want to be reminding him. But it was too late.

'Yeah, I know,' he said. 'You're right. It can't be a clue to where my mum is, because she hadn't gone missing when Sonya wrote this.'

He suddenly looked all miserable again and his eyes sort of clouded over. I wanted to give him a hug, but I couldn't do that, so instead I gave him a pat on the arm and I said, 'We'll think of something, Hal. We will. We'll find her.'

That was complete nonsense. We hadn't the first clue how to go about it. This thing on the piece of paper might mean something, but whatever it meant, it wasn't a clue to the mystery of Hal's missing mother.

Hal sniffled a bit. 'I better be getting home. He'll be wondering what's keeping me.'

'Oh well,' I said. 'Yeah. Better not keep old Shiny Face in suspense, eh?'

Hal sighed. 'I wish I hadn't done it,' he said. 'The hospital thing. I really wish I had never thought of it.'

I didn't know what to say. I wished I was grown up and could think of something soothing, but the only things that came into my head were either stupid or funny. That's the trouble with my head, it's always full of stupid, funny stuff.

Hal kicked himself. I mean, he did literally; he kicked the instep of one foot with the toe of the other. It looked as if it hurt.

'It was supposed to solve a problem,' he said, 'but it only made it worse.'

Chapter 16

I woke up very early the next morning. I don't know what woke me, but the first thing that popped into my head was shoes, shining like polished brown chestnuts. I wondered where that thought had come from, it's weird the way things drift into your mind when you are between sleep and waking, and then I remembered that was what Hal had said to Sonya, something about remembering his dad's shoes. I think he meant on the day he died, but that didn't seem to make a lot of sense. I mean, people don't usually have their shoes on when they die, do they? Unless they have an accident, I suppose. Or drop dead. And why would you notice their shoes? If someone died, you wouldn't be looking at their *feet*, would you? I suppose if you are only five or something, you might be closer to their feet than other people. That didn't seem like a very convincing explanation, though.

Poor Hal, I thought, just like my mother always

says, only I really meant it. I'd never thought about Hal's dad being dead before as, like, a major problem or anything; it was just a fact, especially since it had happened a long time ago, but now I realized, all of a sudden, that my mother was right, and it was awfully sad for Hal, and that was why she always said 'Poor Hal'. That was what the thing about the shoes made me think.

Then I remembered about Hal's mother being missing still, and I lay there for a while and worried about that. Then I wondered why Alec's face was so shiny. After that I wondered if he could de-shine it by using some sort of stuff on it, but that would probably count as make-up and I didn't think he'd be into that idea. I began to feel a bit sorry for him. I mean, not only did he have a shiny face to contend with, but the situation about Hal's mother must be pretty terrible for him as well as for Hal. Plus he also had Hal to worry about.

The next thing I thought was, they really ought to ring the police. I could see that they didn't want to get Trudy into trouble and all, but still, there's a limit, and I would think being missing for nearly a week was definitely it.

Then I thought, without meaning to think it, it just sort of drifted into my head as a fully formed sentence: well, if they aren't going to ring the police, it's up to me to do it.

Me! I thought then. I could hear my own voice

in my head. It was squeaky with terror. What's it got to do with me? I reasoned. It's not my problem. I'm not going to go there.

I turned over and tried to go back to sleep. But having thought such a thought, I couldn't unthink it. I knew I was going to have to act on it.

In the end, I got out of bed. It was nearly six o'clock. If I was lucky, Sonya might still be on the same shift she'd been doing on Saturday, and that would mean she'd be on in the morning. Maybe she'd be there already, if she was due to finish at lunchtime.

I put my dressing gown on and went down to the hall, where the phone book is kept, and I looked up Balnamara Garda station in the green pages where all the official stuff is. It took a while, but I found it. Then I grabbed the cordless phone off its cradle and punched in the number. I ran back upstairs with the phone while it was ringing, and I was back in bed by the time it was answered.

'No,' said a cross-sounding voice, 'Guard O'Rourke is not on duty today.'

'Oh!' I said. 'When will she be in?'

'I can't be giving out that sort of information,' said the cross guard. 'If it's Garda business, you can speak to me. If it's a personal call, you'll have to ring her at home. Is it personal?'

'I suppose so,' I said.

I meant it was personal in the sense that it was

kind of private, not that I wanted to ask her to a party or something, but he didn't give me a chance to explain that.

'Well then,' he said, 'you'll have to make your own arrangements. I can't be spending Garda time talking to you. Slán.' And he hung up.

'Slán,' I said automatically, though he couldn't hear me.

They worry a lot about their time, the guards, don't they?

Chapter 17

The phone leapt in my hand. Well, that's what it felt like. I don't suppose it actually did leap, but anyway, it rang as I sat up in bed with it in my hand.

Maybe he's sorry, I thought, that cross guard. Maybe he's ringing back to apologize. They probably have one of those screens that tells you who's ringing you so you can call them back if you like. We haven't got one of those. We are very lo-tech in this family. My parents think that is a grand thing; I think it's just a pain. We wouldn't even have a cordless phone only the old phone died and it was cheaper to get one of these as a replacement.

But it wasn't the guard: it was Hal.

'Hal!' I yelped. 'It's the middle of the night.'

'Not really,' Hal said. 'It's that sort of plum-coloured time, about six.'

'Does it taste like plums too?' I asked.

'No, mint,' he said. 'Did I wake you? Sorry.'

I wondered if six o'clock in the evening was the same colour and taste, but I didn't get a chance to ask.

'I just wanted to tell you,' Hal went on, 'Alec looked up that quing-ming-jay thing on the computer, I mean, on the Internet. He's an inso-maniac.'

Alec! That was the first time Hal'd ever called his stepfather by his name. But I was a bit distracted by that other thing he had called him.

'Inso *what*?' I asked.

'Maniac,' he repeated. 'Inso-maniac. It means he doesn't sleep.'

'Oh!' I said. 'You mean insomniac.'

'Yes,' said Hal. 'That's what I said. So he gets up early and goes surfing. We have broadband, did I tell you?'

'Hal, do you know that it's six *a.m.*?'

He didn't answer; he just kept going.

'It turns out it's not "queuing" *or* "king" *or* "kwing". It's "ching". That's how you pronounce it. He woke me up to show me this site he found, all about it. It's dead interesting.'

'Ching?' I said. '*Ching!* Oh!' Something was fluttering in my brain. Things were slotting into place. I wasn't sure exactly what things, but something was definitely going on in my head. 'Hal! That must be . . . Hal, is it *Chinese*?'

'That's right,' he said. He sounded a bit

disappointed that I'd worked it out for myself. 'How did you guess?'

'It's that festival, isn't it?' I said, finally realizing the connections that my brain was making. 'That thing in China with the kites, right?'

'Oh!' he said. 'You *knew*. Qing Ming Jie, yes, the Festival of Pure Brightness. How did you know?'

Well, of course, I hadn't known; it was just the only Chinese thing I'd ever heard of apart from wonton soup and dragons and Beijing, and anyway the person who'd mentioned it was Sonya, and she was also the person who'd written those words on the scrap of paper, so it all had to be connected, hadn't it?

I didn't say any of this to Hal. Instead, I said, 'But so what?'

'So that's what Sonya was *saying* to me; she wanted me to know about this festival.'

'Yeah, but what *about* it?'

'I don't know,' Hal said. 'I'm thinking about it, though.'

'Hmm,' I said.

My eyes were starting to prickle with sleep. I'm not usually functioning at six o'clock in the morning.

'It's deadly,' Hal was saying now. 'There's loads of information on this site. It's also called Tomb Sweeping Day.'

'What is?'

'The Festival of Pure Brightness.'

'Tomb sweeping! How do you mean, tomb sweeping?'

'People visit graves and sweep them.'

He's flipped, I thought to myself. He's finally flipped. If I thought he was weird before, that was nothing compared to this.

'Why?'

'I don't know, to tidy them up, I suppose. It's a bit like Halloween, I think, only in the spring. It's about dead people.'

Dead people, that's just terrific, I thought. As if Hal hadn't got enough problems.

'Maybe that's why witches have broomsticks,' I said. 'For sweeping graves.'

'It's not spooky,' Hal said. 'It's in the spring. It's fun.'

Well, if sweeping graves was Hal's idea of fun, he was weirder than I thought.

But the weirdest thing of all was the way Hal was suddenly chattering away about Alec, as if they were old mates. The man he couldn't even say 'Pass the sugar, please' to last week.

'Tell me, Hal,' I said, 'how are you getting on with Alec these days?'

'Eh, well, I dunno, I –'

'Put it this way,' I said. 'Have you put any pebbles in his shoes lately?'

'Um,' he said, 'no. I sort of – went off that idea.'

'That's good,' I said. 'Is he, you know, looking after you properly and everything?'

'Well, I suppose – yeah. He cooks, you know. And washes. He'd washed my school sweatshirt; that's why I couldn't find it.'

'Oh, so *that's* why you had your blue one on.'

'Yeah, he noticed I'd got toothpaste on it, so he put it in the wash. He thought I'd have a spare. It's dry now. I'll be able to wear it today.'

Well, well, well, I thought to myself. Alec *noticed* toothpaste on Hal's sweatshirt and he *washed* it. Curiouser and curiouser. And Hal must have shown that piece of paper to Alec, the one with the Chinese words on it, his precious clue from Sonya. That sounded as if they were practically pally, didn't it? And then Alec had gone to the trouble of looking it up for him. He'd woken Hal up at the crack of dawn to show him some Internet site he'd found. Thick as thieves they were.

Then I had another thought. A tiny suspicion of a thought. About Hal's mum. About what was going on. Thick as thieves. Maybe – could it be? – maybe that was the *whole plan*. It couldn't possibly be true, could it? And yet . . . I'd need to think it through, but it was the only thing that made sense. In the meantime, I wouldn't ring the police just yet. I'd wait and see.

'I'll see you at school, Hal,' I said. 'But now I

really have to catch a bit more sleep before it's time to get up.'

'Yeah,' he said. 'Sorry I woke you, I was just excited. See you later.'

Chapter 18

Larry's tattoo began to fade. I noticed it at breakfast. At first I thought I was just bleary-eyed, after being awake so early, but even after I'd blinked and rubbed my eyes, it was still very fuzzy-looking.

'Larry!' I shrieked. 'Your tattoo, it's disappearing.'

He grinned.

Something had happened to Larry since he'd been to Paris. Things didn't seem to get him down so easily. Maybe he'd fallen in love. I hoped so. I am dying for him to fall in love, because I want to see what it looks like when a boy is in love, so I will know what to watch out for if anyone falls in love with me. When I am older, of course. I don't think I am quite ready to be fallen in love with yet.

Mum was doing something at the sink. I could see her spine stiffening, but she didn't turn round.

'Tattoos *can't* fade,' I said. 'They're there for life, under your skin. They cheated you, Larry; it's a dud. You were done! You are such a twit.'

Mum half-turned at that, one hand raised and covered in soap suds, the other one still in the sink.

'It's not a dud,' Larry said. 'It's a Mehendi design. It's *supposed* to fade.'

'Me-what?' said Mum. 'What's that?'

She dried her hands and came over to us at the table.

'It's an Indian thing,' Larry said. He had rolled up his cuff and was examining the fading design. 'They do it with henna.'

'Henna?' I asked. 'Like for hair?'

'Yes. They squeeze this squidgy stuff out of a sort of icing-bag thingy and it goes hard, like icing, and then they scrape it off. There was this place in Paris that does it, and all the girls were getting themselves covered in leaves and flowers and things. It's mostly girls that get them done, but they dared me to get one done as well, so I did, for a laugh. It's only temporary, Ma.'

'Oh!' Mum said and she sat down with a thunk.

'If you were a Mehendi design, Mum, would you be a flowery one or an animaly one?' I asked her.

She glared at me. I was only trying to be light-hearted. Seems I can say nothing right these days.

'Animaly, I'd say,' I said under my breath. 'A *dragon*.'

'But why did you let me think it was a real

tattoo, Larry?' Mum was almost wailing. 'What you put me through!' She put her head in her hands, as if she had the most appalling children in the world. She does exaggerate, even if it's only by gestures.

'I never said a word!' Larry protested. 'You just started moaning and freaking out. You didn't give me a chance to say anything.'

'But you could have explained.'

Larry shrugged. 'Yeah, well, now you know,' he said.

'And there isn't a hasp in the house,' I added.

Larry grinned. My mother frowned.

'You two,' she said, but she never did add what it was about us two.

I had a sudden moment of inspiration. Why had I not thought of it before? It was staring me in the face and it just hadn't occurred to me. Here was Mrs Psychology sitting in front of me and I hadn't thought of tapping into her great wisdom.

'Mum,' I said. 'I need your advice.'

She stared at me, as if I had said, 'Mum, there's a large pink elephant with green ears standing behind you and it's about to *eat* your apron.'

'You want my advice?' she said wonderingly. 'Why, certainly, Olivia, what's the problem?'

I should ask for her advice more often, I thought. It makes her happy.

'It's to do with Hal,' I said.

'Ah, poor Hal,' she said. I might have known that's what she'd say. 'Tell me about it.'

So I did. We had quite a long chat, as it happens. A very interesting long chat.

Chapter 19

I wasn't looking forward to seeing Hal. I was going to have to tell him the truth or at least make him work out the truth for himself. And it wasn't going to be easy.

He was wearing his proper school sweatshirt that day, and he was looking almost cheerful. His face was pinker than it had been for a long time, and roundier. How was I going to tell him what was really going on?

'I told him,' he announced at break.

This threw me. '*What?* What did you tell who?' I asked. 'I mean whom. Whom did you tell what?'

'Alec. About Saturday. I feel much better about it now that I've owned up.'

That gave me a bit of encouragement. I'd feel better too in a minute, I told myself. It was just a case of doing it and then it would be all much better. Or not. That was the problem. It might be all much worse.

'What about Saturday?' I asked evasively.

'About the mortuary and the paint and everything. About how it was really us.'

'And what did he say?'

'He laughed,' Hal said triumphantly. He smacked the flat of his hand down on a desk – we were in the classroom that break, because it was raining outside. 'He laughed and laughed. He said I was a gas ticket. He said it was the best prank he'd heard of in a long time. It reminded him of the old days, when kids had spirit.'

'So you didn't explain that you did it on purpose to create a row between him and your mother?' I thought I'd better mention his mother before he went off on some other track.

'Eh, no, I didn't think I needed to go that far.'

'And now you're friends, you and Alec?' Well, that would be something. At least the plan would have worked.

'I wouldn't say *friends* exactly,' Hal said cautiously.

'But you're not enemies?'

'Yeah, I suppose we're not.'

'Well then,' I said, relieved. 'All you need to do now is find some way to let your mother know that you two've worked things out and I'd say she'll come galloping back, won't she, all delighted?'

'How do you mean – let her know? – galloping back? – delighted? What are you talking about, Olivia? She's *missing*, remember?'

I gritted my teeth. I was going to have to do this.

'Hal, it's staring you in the face. Think about it. You can't really believe she left home because she was angry about Alec not going to the golf. How daft is that?'

(This is what my mother had said at breakfast, but it was exactly what I'd been starting to think myself.)

'Eh –'

'On a scale of one to ten, Hal, how likely is it that a woman would storm out of the house and leave her only child with a person-not-his-father and not come back for *five whole days* just because the person-not-his-father wouldn't go to a golf tournament? I mean, is this reasonable behaviour?'

'Eh,' he said again. 'When you put it like that –'

'On a scale of one to ten, Hal, how likely? Assuming the woman is your mother, who, let's face it, is not exactly given to grossly irresponsible behaviour. I mean, she's not a raving alcoholic or anything, is she? Or completely crackers?'

'But she might have had an accident,' Hal said. 'She might have lost her memory. She might have been kidnapped. Or arrested. She might be sick.'

'On a scale of one to ten, Hal,' I said firmly.

He caved in. 'Um, about two, I suppose.'

'Right, so when you get a likelihood score of two out of ten for anything, Hal, what would you think?'

Hal squirmed a bit and looked doubtful, but he was following me, I could see.

'I'd think – maybe there was some other explanation?' he said.

The penny hadn't quite dropped, but I could see it was starting to hover on the edge; it was losing its footing.

'Now you're talking,' I said. 'And listen, think about this too: how likely would you think it is that your stepfather would sit around for days, doing nothing about finding your mother, if she was truly missing? Do you think he'd just drift along washing sweatshirts and cooking waffles and not bothering to report her as a missing person? I mean, for one thing, he'd be under suspicion for murder if she didn't turn up.'

'Mu-u-urder?' squeaked Hal. He was white as sliced pan.

'She hasn't been murdered, Hal. That's not what I'm saying. I'm just saying *if* . . .'

'So what's going on?' asked Hal.

I leaned over and whispered in his ear, 'It's a conspiracy, Hal.'

'What? You mean, she's been kidnapped by a – a *consortium*?'

'Hal, you have an overactive imagination. Of course not. The conspiracy is between the pair of them. Alec and Trudy.'

'Alec and my ma? What sort of a conspiracy?'

This was heavy going.

'A conspiracy to bring someone to his senses.'

'Who?' said Hal.

'You know who,' I persisted.

'Me?' said Hal and he pointed his finger into his chest, as if he thought I mightn't know who 'me' was in this case. He screwed the finger around, as if he was trying to make sure he was really there.

'You,' I said and I jabbed my finger into his chest as well.

The bell rang.

'But that's . . .' said Hal.

'Hal!' rapped Kate as she came bustling in. 'The bell has rung. Put away your lunch box now, no more talking. Sit down. I mean, sit up. Take out your workbooks. Pay attention.'

'. . . *cruel*,' Hal finished in a whisper.

Chapter 20

I would have thought he'd be delighted, Hal, but he's not exactly your normal chap, is he? I thought he'd fall on my neck, like that fellow in the Bible, and say, 'Thank you, Olivia, you have shown me the truth,' or something. But there is no pleasing some people.

He frowned his way through the day and I could see he wasn't listening to a single thing Kate said, and when school was over he stomped off out the door without even waiting for me, like he usually does.

'Hal!' I called after him. 'Wait for me!'

So he did, but he didn't turn round and smile or wave or anything. He just stood where he stopped and waited for me, and as soon as I'd caught up with him, he started striding ahead again.

'Don't shoot the messenger, Hal,' I said breathlessly as I trotted along, trying to keep up with him. 'I mean, it's not *my* fault if your mum has taken extreme measures to make you see sense.'

'I'm not,' Hal said. 'I'm just thinking.'

'You've been thinking all day,' I said. 'I could almost hear you, you were thinking so hard.'

He didn't say anything to that.

'If you were a think tank,' I said, 'would you be a panzer or one of those glass jobs for fish?'

'What are you wittering about, Olivia?'

'Think tanks,' I said. 'I am trying to imagine what it is like to be in one, and I am wondering if yours is full of water or what.'

'It's not that kind of tank,' Hal said. 'That's just a metaphor.'

'Oh very good, Hal,' I said. He does listen to me sometimes, even if he doesn't look as if he's listening.

'It's full of thoughts,' Hal said.

'Are they good ones?'

'They are confusing,' Hal said.

'But good all the same?' I persisted.

I mean, I had more or less pointed out to him that his mother wasn't lying in a ditch being nibbled by the rats, and she had not eloped to Tasmania with the postman either. She was probably in, oh, I don't know, Clondalkin, maybe, or Nobber, someplace within a couple of hours' drive anyway, waiting for Hal and Alec to work things out to the point where she could come back and they could start to live like a proper family, where people do not try to get each other arrested on a Saturday morning. That's what my mother had said anyway, and she should know, because . . .

'Olivia!' Hal suddenly stopped walking and turned round to me. I almost bumped into him.

'What?' I said.

'Welcome to the think tank,' he said. 'Listen, sit down for a minute.' And he sat down himself, right there, on the footpath, on the kerb I mean, with his feet in the gutter. He lifted his bottom and shoved his school bag under it, so he had a sort of cushion, and then he clasped his hands round his knees.

I didn't really want to sit in the gutter, but I put my school bag down too and sat beside him. School bags make very knobbly cushions.

'Well?' I said expectantly.

'This theory you have,' he said, 'about my mum not being really missing?'

'It's not a theory, Hal. It's true.'

'How can you say that?' he said. 'How can you possibly know?'

'Because . . .' Was he ready to hear this? I wondered. But I plunged ahead anyway. He had to know. It couldn't go on like this. It wasn't fair. 'Because *my* mum says so.'

'Oh, and how does your mum know what my mum is doing?'

'They work together, Hal.'

'So?'

'Hal – your mother . . . has been at work . . . every day this week,' I said. 'My mother told me.'

Hal jumped up off his school bag as if it was on fire and stared down at me. Then he paced away from me, with his hands in his pockets. Then he paced back. He flailed his arms about in the air, like a demented windmill. Finally, he sat down beside me again. He looked as if he was going to explode, but I didn't know if it was with joy at knowing his mum was alive, or with anger at her for putting him through this or irritation with me for – well, I don't know what I was supposed to have done wrong.

'Tell me that again,' he said, through half-clenched teeth.

'My mum says . . . she told me at breakfast this morning . . . she says, of course your mum is not missing. She *knows* your mum is not missing, because . . . because . . . oh, Hal, she's been at work every day this week and she hasn't said a word about not being at home. It's all some big put-up job, Hal.'

I said the last bit very quietly, the way you tiptoe around when someone is sick or upset. You don't want to make it worse. But still it was good news overall. His mum was alive and she might even be coming home.

'But she hasn't been at home,' Hal insisted. He couldn't take it in.

'Well, no, obviously not,' I said. 'I don't imagine she is hiding under the stairs until you go to bed at night and then creeping out for a sandwich.'

Hal gave a crooked little grin at that. Then he frowned and said, 'But why didn't you tell me before now, Olivia?'

'I've been trying,' I said. 'It's hard to find the right words. I only heard this morning when I spoke to my mum about it.'

He put his elbows on his knees and his head in his hands and he started to rock back and forth. I wasn't sure if he was actually crying. I looked around. Nobody was about, so very gingerly I put my hand out and I patted his back. He went on rocking, and I went on patting, and after a while he stopped rocking and I stopped patting, but I left my hand there, resting between his shoulder blades, and after a moment he turned his body round to me and without a word he put his head on my shoulder, like a great big soppy Labrador or something, and I brought my other hand round and stroked his hair and we sat there like that for a little while and it was dead nice.

After a bit he lifted his head and looked at me and I thought it might be no harm to give him a little smile, so I did, and he gave this huge sigh and I could feel it under my hand running right through him.

'If you were a friend, Olivia,' he whispered,

'would you be a best mate or just a good pal?'

'I'd be someone who loves you, Hal,' I said.

I don't know what made me say it. I nearly died of embarrassment as soon as it was out. I could feel myself blushing like mad, but Hal just grinned a bit and said, 'You're deadly, Olivia,' so I knew it was OK; he didn't think I was *proposing* to him or anything.

Eventually, we drew apart and we stood up and put our school bags on our backs again and walked on, side by side.

'What'll you do now, Hal?' I asked as we came to my gate. 'Will you tell Alec the game is up, you know she's not really lost and ask him to ask her to come back, all is forgiven et cetera?'

'Well,' said Hal. 'Something like that maybe. I'll have to think about it. I'll phone you later.'

'OK, Hal,' I said.

I wondered if he expected me to give him a little kiss or something, which was definitely not in my immediate plans, but I didn't really think he did, so I just grabbed his hand for a moment and gave his fingers a tiny squeeze, and he squeezed back and I knew everything was fine.

'See you, Hal,' I said and I went inside.

Chapter 21

Hal didn't phone. Instead, he came round, with his famous kite, to see if I'd come to the Low Strand with him. We were just finishing our dinner, and my mum asked him to sit down and have a bowl of ice cream with us.

'Is that OK, Dad?' I asked, meaning about going to the Low Strand, and he said no, not on a weekday, not at that time of the evening, but I said, 'Da-ad,' and I stepped hard on his toe under the table and jiggled my eyebrows at him so he would get the message that this wasn't any old day in Hal's life.

Of course, he didn't get it, but Mum noticed and she piped up, 'Oh, Paul, I think it'd be OK just for once.'

My father swung round to my mother, clearly put out that she wasn't toeing the agreed parental line, but then she started at the eyebrow-wiggling too. My parents are OK, really, I have to say. I mean, there is room for improvement, but as parents go, they are in the honours class, I'd say.

Suddenly there was this horrible noise, like a cat stuck in a washing machine. Actually, I have never heard a cat in a washing machine, but I imagine it would sound like that.

'What's that?' I squawked.

'It's my phone,' Hal said, picking it up from the table where he'd left it. It had been throwing a fit, making as if to jump off on to the floor. 'It's on vibrate.'

'It sounds like . . .' But I didn't get a chance to tell him about the cat in the washing machine.

'Oh hi, *Mammy*!' he yelled. 'Oh hello, hello, oh, Ma!'

It was his mother.

He waved at me and mouthed something I couldn't understand. Then suddenly there were these great big globs of tears running down his face.

'OK,' he sobbed. 'OK, OK, OK. Yes. OK. Yes. Great. OK.'

Eventually, he stopped nodding and saying yes and great and OK and pressed the red key.

'She's alive,' he said, with this huge grin across his face.

'I know,' I said. 'I told you. Did you not believe me?'

'Of course I did, but to hear her voice . . .' and he started blubbering again.

My poor dad didn't know what was going on. He doesn't like not knowing what is going on; it makes him jittery. He started humming, always a sure sign.

'Well,' I said, 'I'm glad she's alive. I wouldn't be a bit happy if she was phoning you from Beyond the Grave.'

Larry let out a strangulated snort, which I think was him trying not to laugh and not completely succeeding.

Hal wiped his face with the back of his cuff. I never let on I'd noticed he'd been crying.

'She's coming home tonight,' he said. He turned to my dad. 'Could you see your way to letting Olivia come with me for a little while? I'll bring her back safely. Before dark. Please?'

My mother was twitching everything on her face, ears, nose, everything, and nodding like mad at him, so he stopped humming, sighed and said, 'Well, be home by half-past nine at the very latest.'

We grabbed the kite and off we went.

Chapter 22

'Well, what happened?' I asked when we were on the way. We were walking, because it's too awkward to cycle with the kite.

'After school today?' he said. 'What happened was I went home.'

'Yes, and?'

'And Alec came home after work as usual.'

'And?'

'And I just said what you told me to say.'

'Give me the exact words, Hal,' I ordered. I wanted to get a clear picture of what had happened.

'"Listen, Alec, I think we can safely say the experiment has succeeded. So maybe it's time you rang my mother and told her it would be OK if she came home now. I'm sure you know where she is."'

I nearly choked. 'Was he astonished?' I asked.

'I don't know,' said Hal, 'because I just threw it over my shoulder as I was leaving the room. I didn't say another word and he never answered.'

'But he must have done it? Considering your mother rang you there just now.'

'Yeah, he must have, mustn't he?'

'So why are we going to the strand? Do you not want to be at home when your mum comes back? You must be dying to see her.'

'Hmm,' said Hal. 'It's like this, I have something to do and I want to do it now. She'll be there when I get back. I'd say *she'll* be dying to see *me*, won't she?'

'Oh yeah, I'd say,' I said.

'But it was a mean trick,' he said. 'It was a dirty rotten thing to do to me. To think of how totally miserable I have been!'

'Well, it wasn't very nice,' I agreed. 'But I suppose she was desperate. Are you going to forgive her?'

'Yes,' he said. 'I've been thinking about it. I have to really. She's my mother. You only have one of those. But all the same . . .'

I kind of knew what he meant. It was a terrible thing to do to him. It had worked, though. It had made him and Alec rub along together. She'd got what she wanted. Poor Hal. He had to give in. He didn't have any choice.

'So . . . are they going to get married then?' I asked him.

'Oh, I suppose so,' Hal said. 'They can if they want to. What difference does it make at this stage?

But they are not going to get away with packing me off to boarding school. They can forget about that one.' He sounded very fierce.

'It might be fun, though. You might enjoy it. And there might be one where you could play, oh, volleyball or something. If you'd prefer that.'

'Hmm,' Hal said. 'Well, we'll see. But they are not going to *make* me go if I don't want to, that's for sure.'

'That's right, Hal,' I said. 'You tell them!'

Well, you can just imagine who was at the strand when we got there, can't you? Old Tweedle. He's practically a permanent fixture, I'd say, like St Peter at the gates of heaven.

He raised his hat at us as he bustled by with his tiny dog. I wasn't sure if he was just being polite or if he remembered us from before, when he gave us all the advice about the kite.

Hal unravelled the kite slowly as he walked and I strolled along beside him. It was nearly eight, but still very light. That's the good thing about June: the afternoon goes on all evening. I stopped to unstrap my sandals and take them off. Hal had already let the kite off by the time I caught up with him again.

The wind was slight and the kite bobbed uncertainly for a while in mid-air. I looked around while Hal worked on getting it to rise. Tweedledee-dumbunter had stopped to watch. I think he must have recognized us after all.

Then Hal gave a certain twitch to the string and the kite started to mount the blue air. It hung for a moment, above our heads, its two gorgeous tails dangling straight down. The bright red border etched its shape against the sea and sky, as Hal had meant it to do, and then the breeze lifted it higher and it turned lazily, like a swimmer lying back to float, and the tails were glorious, multi-coloured streamers, flying along almost horizontal now behind it.

Higher it went and higher, so high my neck ached with watching it. I wished I could fly with it, way out over the sea and look down on all the countryside. Higher, higher, I'd never seen it climb so high before.

I turned to Hal and said, 'Look how high it is; it's way, way up in the sky. I didn't think the string was that long.'

'It isn't,' he said and he held out empty hands.

He'd let go of the string.

'Hal! Your lovely kite! You've lost it!'

I grabbed one of his hands, to comfort him, but he was smiling. 'No,' he said, 'I haven't lost it.' He hung on to my hand all the same. 'I've *sent* it, up into the blue.'

'Why?' I asked. 'Why, after all your trouble with it? Why did you just let it go?'

I have to admit I had a little twinge of worry on behalf of the environment too. I mean, if people went around letting off kites . . . But then I thought, well, I suppose they don't really, do they?

'It was Sonya's idea,' he said, 'in a way.'

'Have you been talking to *Sonya*?' I yelped.

He swung my arm and we ran a few excited steps along the strand. Then we stopped and continued to crane and squint at the sky. The kite was still visible, but only just as a streak of colour now.

'No,' he said, in answer to my question. 'I just mean, I solved the clue she gave me.'

'I don't get it, Haldane,' I said.

He laughed because I'd called him by his full first name and he swung my arm again. He was smiling all over his face. All over his body, almost.

'On Qing Ming Jie,' he said, 'you know, the Festival of Pure Brightness, people sometimes let go of their kites; they let them sail up into the heavens, to the realm of the ancestors.'

'The ancestors?'

'The dead people. The ones who have died before us. The ones whose children we are.'

'Why?' I asked.

'It's a kind of present, like the statue to the poet in the square.'

'Oh!' I said. It began to make sense. A bit of sense, anyway.

'I knew the kite had to be blue,' he said. 'I knew that all along. But I couldn't work out why.'

'And now you know why?'

He didn't answer. 'It's free now, Olivia. Look, it's on its way,' he said softly, and we both stood for a few moments and watched as the tiny coloured speck finally disappeared into the blue of the sky. 'And now it's just blue,' Hal said. 'Like Friday.'

Glossary

a-lanna my child (anglicization of Gaelic *leanbh*, used as a term of endearment to a girl)

Balnamara fictional seaside town (anglicization of Gaelic *Baile na Mara* or *Béal na Mara*, sea town or mouth of the sea)

ban-gharda (Gaelic) female police officer. This term is no longer considered correct, but people do use it in everyday speech when they want to distinguish a female police officer from a male one.

boreen narrow, untarred road (anglicization of Gaelic *bóithrín*, literally 'little road')

Garda the Irish police force (abbreviation of Gaelic *Garda Síochána*, literally 'Peace Guard')

garda police officer (Gaelic word for 'guard'; plural: *gardaí*)

guard police officer (English translation,

often used colloquially instead of *garda*)

(the) guards (the) police

Kimberley a lightly spiced sandwich biscuit with a marshmallow filling, popular in Ireland

Mikado a pink coconut marsh-mallow biscuit with a jam filling, popular in Ireland

rath barrow, ancient burial mound, fairy fort

runners trainers, running shoes

SESE social, environ-mental and scientific education, a subject on the primary school curriculum in Ireland

slán (Gaelic) goodbye

sliced pan sliced loaf bread

TG4 popular Irish-language television station

ye/yiz you, plural (colloquial or dialect)

Author's note

The picture that Olivia saw with her parents – the one where she imagined the people might be flying kites (though, in fact, they are not) – is called 'A Sunday Afternoon on the Island of La Grande Jatte'. It was painted by the French artist Georges Seurat in the years 1884 to 1886.

Jake likes thinking, talking, football and encyclopedias.

And fish. But he's not so sure about everything else – especially girls, or little sisters, or stepdads. And most of all, he's not sure if he really likes himself.

Discover

Something Invisible

the irresistible new novel from bestselling and award-winning Siobhán Parkinson.

Puffin by Post

Blue Like Friday – Siobhán Parkinson

If you have enjoyed this book and want to read more, then check out these other great Puffin titles. You can order any of the following books direct with Puffin by Post:

Second Fiddle • Siobhán Parkinson • 9780141318806	£4.99
Does friendship always come first?	

Something Invisible • Siobhán Parkinson • 9780141318837	£4.99
'An exquisitely wise story of love, loss and too many sisters' – Meg Rosoff, author of *How I Live Now* and *Just in Case*	

Driftwood • Cathy Cassidy • 9780141320212	£5.99
'Cassidy's characters have real heart' – *Sunday Telegraph*	

Cross Your Heart, Connie Pickles • Sabine Durrant • 9780141319407	£5.99
'A dream of a read' – *Observer*	

Once • Morris Gleitzman • 9780141320632	£5.99
'Poignant and memorable' – *Guardian*	

Just contact:

Puffin Books, C/o Bookpost, PO Box 29,
Douglas, Isle of Man, IM99 1BQ
Credit cards accepted. For further details:
Telephone: 01624 677237
Fax: 01624 670923

You can email your orders to: bookshop@enterprise.net
Or order online at: www.bookpost.co.uk

Free delivery in the UK.
Overseas customers must add £2 per book.

Prices and availability are subject to change.

Visit puffin.co.uk to find out about the latest titles, read extracts and exclusive author interviews, and enter exciting competitions. You can also browse thousands of Puffin books online.